EROS

CUPID'S CAPTIVE, BOOK ONE

Eva Pohler

Copyright © 2019 by Eva Pohler.

Eva Pohler Books
20011 Park Ranch
San Antonio, Texas 78259
www.evapohler.com

Publisher's Note: This is a work of fiction. Names, characters, places, and incidents are a product of the author's imagination. Locales and public names are sometimes used for atmospheric purposes. Any resemblance to actual people, living or dead, or to businesses, companies, events, institutions, or locales is completely coincidental.

Book Layout ©2017 BookDesignTemplates.com

Book Cover Design by Keri Knutson

Eros/ Eva Pohler. -- 1st ed.
Paperback ISBN: 978-1-958390-61-0

The Olympians deserve a day of reckoning.

—HADES

Contents

For my husband.

Mothers

The drizzle over Oklahoma City hadn't dissuaded fans from packing the stadium below, where the Women's College World Series had just ended.

Eros, better known as Cupid, hovered in the summer clouds beside Aphrodite above the celebrating team and its fans, wondering why his mother had brought him here. His golden curls clung to his face, damp from the drizzle, in the same way that his mother's hair clung to her neck and shoulders. He pulled his hands from the pockets of his trousers to straighten his bowtie, which was also damp and probably ruined.

Beneath her breath, Aphrodite said, "Enjoy your victory while you can. You aren't long for this world, number thirty-two."

Cupid scanned the players below. "Who's number thirty-two?"

Aphrodite put her hands on her hips—a gesture he'd come to associate with anger. Even in her long blue gown and heels, she could be intimidating. "That makes *one* person who hasn't heard of her. Come on, Darling. Her name has been on the lips of every mortal in America for months."

Cupid lifted his palms and shook his head.

Aphrodite nearly spit when she said, "Ellie Beaufort."

Cupid *had* heard of her. He'd received countless prayers from young men and women who'd apparently fallen in love with her. He now understood his mother's annoyance. The less she was worshipped, the weaker her powers became. It was true of all the gods. His best strategy was to downplay and distract. "She's an exceptional athlete, Mother. Nothing more."

The goddess of love glared at the field below, where number thirty-two sat perched on the shoulders of her teammates, laughing with glee. "She does have a certain *je ne sais quoi* about her, no?"

Cupid knew better than to take his mother's bait. "I don't know what they see in her," he lied.

"They call her a goddess," Aphrodite said. "The most beautiful creature alive."

Ellie Beaufort's black curls draped across her slender shoulders. The chocolate hue of her skin wasn't particularly striking. Her full lips and brown eyes were nothing extraordinary, and although her cheeks were pleasant, especially when she smiled, they weren't so pleasant as to explain the woman's overall beauty. Cupid could not fathom why the sum of such ordinary traits resulted in Ellie's exceptional appearance; but there it was: a thorn in his mother's side.

"Her popularity will soon pass," Cupid said.

Aphrodite shook her head. "I want you to kill her for me."

Back in the stables at Mount Olympus, Cupid commiserated with Pegasus, who had a hurt hindfoot. Two days ago, they had secretly followed Hermes and Hecate to the northeast of Greece to a rushing brook amid rolling hills outside of a tiny village, where Hermes and Hecate liked to fish. The swift messenger god and the goddess of witchcraft, who'd been shot with Cupid's arrows eons ago, shared a deep love but had never acted on it.

This was beyond Cupid's understanding. While it was true that his arrows couldn't *force* love between people, they were powerful enough to overwhelm even the strongest gods and goddesses possessing an iota of desire in their hearts. So why hadn't Hermes and Hecate shared so much as a lover's kiss?

Should I shoot them again? Cupid had asked Pegasus telepathically.

The winged horse had nodded his reply with a wink.

Then Hermes had suddenly straightened his back and had looked around from where he sat on the bank, as if he'd sensed their presence. As Cupid and Pegasus had attempted to fly away, Pegasus's right hind-foot got caught in a crevice. The white horse panicked and tugged when he should have god-traveled. Something in his foot popped, causing Hecate and Hermes to drop their fishing rods and fly toward Pegasus. Cupid had barely managed to god-travel Pegasus and himself away to avoid being discovered.

For two days, Cupid had searched for Apollo, hoping the god would heal the horse, to no avail. Cupid thought the foot would have healed on its own by now, but it was still tender to the touch. In addition, Pegasus had been unable to fly. This could mean only one thing: Hecate had hexed him. If she had done so wittingly, she would have visited them by now, to learn why they'd been spying. Cupid suspected that she'd cast a blind spell, unaware of her victim's identity, but hoping to out a powerless deity.

Fortunately, Pegasus hadn't been summoned by Zeus and had managed to hide out in the stables.

"Don't worry," Cupid reassured his friend. "I'll find Apollo. Meanwhile, your powers should come back anytime now."

He was only speculating. There was no knowing how long Hecate's hex would last.

Cupid gave the horse's flank a final stroke before flying away.

The search for Apollo to help Pegasus had been Cupid's excuse to his mother for putting off the deed she wanted done. He took no pleasure in killing innocent mortals. Over the years, he'd developed a talent for distracting Aphrodite whenever a mortal beauty emerged into global popularity. He'd simply shoot another arrow into his mother's heart in the presence of Ares, Cupid's father, and the two lovers would be off to Paris for months on end, after which, the beauty of the day would have been long forgotten. But, like Apollo, Ares was nowhere to be found. And Aphrodite's patience was thinning.

"What do you want with Apollo?" Artemis asked Cupid, where he'd found her at the edge of her favorite hunting grounds.

"Pegasus has a bad foot that won't heal."

"That's odd."

"Have you seen your brother, or not?"

The goddess shook her head, her brown hair tumbling behind her in the wind, before she fit an arrow to her bow.

Cupid flew away in disgust. Her arrows were not like his. Hers killed innocent beasts.

After hours of questioning the other gods, Cupid abandoned his search and went home, where Psyche was boiling something on the stove.

"Where's Deacon?" Cupid asked of their satyr servant.

"Today's his day off," Psyche said as she added pepper to the pot. "Welcome back."

He loved his wife but not her cooking—though she did look cute in an apron, which she wore tied around her waist over her short red skirt. He patted her bottom and kept his thoughts to himself.

She kissed his cheek. "Your mother came by to see you."

Cupid sighed. "Of course, she did."

"What's got you so agitated, my love?"

Cupid told her about Ellie Beaufort and his mother's wish.

Psyche's emerald eyes widened. "You aren't going to kill her, are you? She might as well be me. Don't you remember? Your mother sent you to kill me for the very same reason."

Cupid kissed her silky dark hair. "I can't marry *every* pretty girl my mother wants dead."

"I'm serious."

"What choice do I have? You know how my mother is."

He worked with his mother nearly every day to carry out the destinies of lovers. She was also his strongest ally, after his father, Ares. It was best to keep his mother happy.

Psyche stirred the boiling pot of what smelled like stew—though the aroma wasn't always an accurate indicator of the pot's contents when Psyche was the cook. "I've never understood how she can be so kind, so loving, and so compassionate one minute and so cruel the next."

"She takes after her father," Cupid said.

Psyche put down her spoon and cupped his face. "Not you. You are nothing but pure love and…"

Her lips were too near his to resist interrupting her with a kiss. He cradled her head as he pressed his mouth, hard, against hers. Her lips were moist, her breath hot. Desire shot through his loins.

"The stew can simmer," Psyche said in between kisses as she pushed him toward their bedroom. "Oh, what you do to me."

He gave her a lustful laugh as he swept her up in his arms and carried her to bed.

"Ellie Beaufort?"

Ellie raised her hand and said, "here," when the professor called her name.

Ellie didn't recognize any of the other twenty or so students in the class. Most of her teammates had gone home for the first few weeks of summer to rest before practice would start up again.

Not Ellie. She was stuck retaking Freshman Comp. And she was a junior.

She supposed she was better off at Florida State than at home, for many reasons—the biggest of which was the unsolicited attention she'd been receiving from the media. She'd already done one commercial for Nike at the urging of her mother. Although Ellie liked the money, she hated being in the limelight. Ellie's coach had said she could protect Ellie from reporters on campus, but she could do nothing for her if Ellie went home.

The other students in the classroom smiled at her. That happened to Ellie a lot. People congratulated her, even though she had no idea who they were. "Good game," they would say, and she would say, "Thanks."

But they rarely said anything else.

Ellie gazed through the window overlooking the fountain, which was empty, probably for maintenance. It was strange how you could be in a crowded room and still feel alone—even when people knew your name.

But Ellie wore her mask, like she always did in public. She took a slow, deep breath, reminding herself that she would get through this, one day at a time. She wouldn't allow herself to consider the alternative, even though it was there, at the edge of her mind, her constant companion.

For Ellie, the softball season couldn't get here fast enough, when she could return to autopilot, where everything came naturally, and she didn't have to think.

As the teacher went over the syllabus, Ellie tried to pay attention, but her head was killing her. All she wanted to do was run. During the off season, she ran every day, listening to her favorite band through her earbuds. She couldn't wait to feel the wind against her face and the sound of Juicy Jenkins wailing out her tunes. For now, Ellie focused on her breathing to help her get through the class. She knew that, with each passing breath, time would pass, and that was the trick of living—to pass the time.

After class, Ellie picked up some food from the cafeteria and carried it back to her dorm, where it was quiet, especially on the third floor, where the softball players lived. Her stomach hurt, but she knew she should eat. She collapsed on the sofa in the living room and set the Styrofoam container on the coffee table, willing herself to open it. When nothing else sounded good, she could usually count on mac and cheese, but even it didn't sound appealing today. Without the distraction of softball, her old friend had returned to torment her.

The voice in her head reminded her that there was no point or purpose. A person was simply alive one day and dead the next, and nothing in between really mattered. The voice made her question why she had come to Florida State. Although some of her classes had been interesting, like psychology and astronomy, most of them seemed like a waste of time. Life in general was a waste of time. Life was a waste. It was nothing. She was nothing.

She stuck the container of food into the refrigerator of the tiny kitchen and went to her bedroom to change into her running shoes. Now that softball season was over, the only way to keep the darkness away was to run.

Before she'd finished tying her laces, her phone vibrated. Ellie glanced at the screen. Her mother was calling.

"Hello, Mom," Ellie said into the phone.

"Where you at?"

"My dorm. Why?"

"I thought you was coming home for a few weeks," her mother said. "Donna told me Shalynn's already home. You were supposed to ride back with her. I can't afford no airplane ride. I got bills."

Shalynn was Ellie's roommate, recruited by Florida State from the same high school in Louisiana.

"I told you, I got summer school."

"Why you got summer school?"

"I failed English. I have to retake it. I told you."

"Dammit, Ellie. I need you here. I was looking forward to a break, you know, from watching Jonivan."

Jonivan was Dominique's son. Dominique was Ellie's sister, who was two year's younger and was a single mom, just like their mother. Dominique got a job at a bank making more money than their mother made cleaning houses, so, except for one client that let her bring the toddler with her, her mother quit her job to babysit Jonivan.

"Well, I'm sorry. I'm stuck here," Ellie said as she rubbed at her temples. The pain in her head had sharpened.

"You won the World Series for that school, and they gonna make you retake English?"

"Mom, it doesn't work like that. Besides, I didn't win it all by myself."

"You sure as hell did. I know you don't believe me, but I watched you on TV. I saw you pitch. Three up and three down. Almost every inning. That was you."

Ellie smiled. Her mother rarely said such things. It felt good. "I still have to pass my classes."

"Are you even trying?"

Ellie frowned. "Yes."

"I'm gonna ask Shalynn if you been skipping classes, and you know her momma gonna make her tell me the truth."

"I don't skip classes, except when I don't feel good."

"Well, hell. That's all the damn time."

Ellie had wanted to say, "Ain't that the truth," but she held her tongue. The doctors hadn't been able to find anything wrong with her, and when one of them had mentioned depression, Ellie's mother had rolled her eyes and had asked, "You mean it's all in her head?"

Ellie sighed. "What do you care if I go to school? You're not paying for it."

"Don't you talk to me like that. I'm still your mother. You got responsibilities here at home."

Taking care of Jonivan was not Ellie's responsibility, but it would do no good to say that out loud. "I gotta go, Mom. I gotta study."

"You be sure and do that. You hear me? Don't be lying to me."

"Goodbye, Mom."

Ellie ended the call and buried her face in her pillow.

CHAPTER TWO

Messengers

The next day after class, while Ellie stood in line for mac and cheese in the cafeteria, Andrew came up to her. Andrew was Shalynn's boyfriend.

"What's up?" he asked, which shocked her, because he never talked to her.

"Hey," Ellie said with a forced smile before turning to the menu mounted above the serving line. She pretended to read it, hoping Andrew would move on.

"A group of us are going out to Landon's Flats tonight," Andrew said.

"Cool."

"It's twenty-cent Tuesday. Twenty-cent drinks all night. You can't beat that deal."

Ellie continued to stare at the menu overhead, moving her lips as she read the food items.

"They a little watered down, but when you can get five for a dollar, why complain?"

She willed the boy to go away.

Andrew rubbed his nose before thrusting his hands into his jean pockets. "You should come."

Ellie tried to hide her surprise. "Yeah, I don't think so."

"What? You too good for us?"

She shook her head, feeling the blood rush to her cheeks. "That ain't it."

"What then?"

"Why do you want me to go anyway, Andrew? You never said two words to me."

"I got a friend wants to meet you. Name's Gabe."

More blood rushed to Ellie's cheeks. "I don't feel so good. Maybe another time."

"My friend, he make you feel real good." Andrew chuckled.

"What does Shalynn think about you going out?"

"She know I can't stay cooped up all summer just 'cause she ain't here."

Ellie supposed that was true. Part of her wanted to go, wanted to say yes to having fun and making new friends; but a bigger part of her just wanted to go home and curl up in bed and play solitaire on her phone until she fell asleep.

"I don't know," she said.

"Think about it. You don't have to decide right this minute."

Ellie nodded, and Andrew gave her another smile before he left.

Back in her room, Ellie played a game on her phone while she forced down her lunch. A voice inside her head told her she needed to get out and have fun—that life was meant to be more than just surviving while you passed the time. Gabe could be cute and smart and nice. Maybe they would hit it off. Maybe a boyfriend could be the answer to her loneliness.

But a louder voice reminded her that she was tired, that she didn't feel good, that she needed rest, and that nothing really mattered, anyway. It said that Gabe was probably a jerk, just like every other guy who'd ever shown interest in her. And if he wasn't a jerk, he probably wouldn't like her, because Ellie wasn't any fun. Her talent as a pitcher was the only thing she had going for her, the voice said. She didn't have anything to talk about with other people or any common interests to share. The voice reminded her that it wouldn't take Gabe long to discover that Ellie was boring, depressing, and prudish.

She was twenty-one, and she'd never been kissed. She'd never even held a boy's hand (second grade didn't count).

Her phone vibrated. It was Shalynn.

"Hey," Ellie said into the phone.

"Hey," Shalynn replied. "What's up?"

"Nothing. What's going on?"

"Andrew said he asked you to go to Landon's Flats tonight. You going?"

Ellie sighed. "I don't know. I don't think so."

"Why not?"

"I'm tired."

"You and me both, girlfriend. That was a hell of a season."

"The best," Ellie said, wishing it hadn't ended.

"I slept 'til noon today. Felt good."

"Wish I could. My class starts at nine-thirty."

"That's not too bad. At least it ain't eight!"

Ellie chuckled. "True."

"I wish you'd go tonight," Shalynn said. "I hear Gabe's really nice."

"You don't know him?"

"Uh-uh. He and Andrew just started hanging out."

"Great. Watch him be a serial killer."

Shalynn laughed. "He ain't a serial killer."

"You don't know that."

"Andrew will have your back. Come on, Ellie. Go tonight. For *me*?"

"Why do you care if I go?"

"I need you to keep an eye on Andrew for me. Make sure he don't get into trouble."

"I thought he was supposed to have my back, not the other way around."

"I'm scared he's gonna meet someone new. At least, if you're there, you can make sure he don't forget about me."

Ellie closed her eyes, feeling the weight of her friend's request. So much pressure.

"Please?" Shalynn asked again.

"I'll think about it. Okay?"

"Thank you, Ellie. Thank you so much!"

"I said I'd think about it. That doesn't mean…"

"I know. I know. I'm just grateful you're doing that. Text me later and let me know what you decide. Okay?"

"All right."

"Love you!"

"Love you, too."

They hung up.

Ellie got up and looked at herself in her bathroom mirror. "Well, hell."

Cupid detested the Underworld and all those who dwelled there, but it was the only place he hadn't searched for Apollo.

He found old Charon on his raft near the massive iron gates, where Cerberus stood guard, towering over the intersection of the Acheron and the River Styx. Cupid remained on the opposite side of the Acheron, not wanting to alarm the three-headed dog. Cupid had learned his lesson the last time he'd approached the gates. It had taken three Furies and the god of sleep to silence the barking heads.

As Thanatos led two souls aboard Charon's raft, Cupid called out from across the river: "Hey, there! Can you help a god out?"

Thanatos was one of two gods with the ability to be in many places at once. While he continued to guide the souls on the raft, another version of him approached Cupid. "Hello, Cupid."

Cupid had rarely spoken to the god of death because his duties were repugnant, but, each time, Cupid had been shocked by his beauty. "Hello, Thanatos. I'm looking for Apollo. Have you seen him?"

"He's gone to Tartarus to talk to Tiresias. Ares is with him."

Cupid lifted his brow in surprise. "I wonder why."

"They didn't say."

"Do you think Hades will let me in, to talk to them?"

"He's in a mood. It's that time of year."

Cupid understood. Persephone was with her mother on Mount Olympus. It was the wrong time of year to ask a favor of Hades. But if Apollo and Ares had been allowed in, why shouldn't Cupid?

"Would you ask him anyway?"

Thanatos nodded. "I'm looking for him now. He's not in his usual place—his sulking chair. Oh, found him. He's in the Seers' Pit with the others."

"What are they up to?"

"I'm not invited in," Thanatos said. "They've asked me to leave. How curious."

"Indeed." Cupid couldn't imagine why the three gods would have a secret meeting with an old seer who spoke in riddles.

Thanatos lifted a finger. "I do know that Apollo and Ares visited the Fates before calling on Tiresias."

"Interesting." Cupid cupped his chin. What in hell was going on?

At that moment, one of Cerberus's heads sniffed Cupid's scent and glared at him from the opposite bank before emitting a low growl.

"You better go," Thanatos warned, "before you get him all riled up."

"Good idea."

Cupid god-traveled away from the gates of the Underworld to the garden in front of his house, pondering what he'd just learned. Situated on a hill just below Mount Olympus, Cupid's castle afforded an amazing view of the heavenly gates above and the Greek countryside below.

From where Cupid stood, he could take in the entirety of the Aegean Sea.

He hadn't chosen this location for purely aesthetic reasons, however. His position made it possible for him to see all who left and entered Mount Olympus. And even though Poseidon's Palace was hidden from view at the bottom of the Aegean, Cupid was sure to notice the moment a chariot emerged from the sea.

Just then, his brothers—Phobos and Deimos—appeared. Identical twins, they were the gods of fear and panic. Cupid filled with dread at the sight of them.

Whereas Cupid had inherited their mother's golden curls, Phobos and Deimos wore the same vibrant red mane as their father, Ares. And while Cupid had a boyish, beardless face, the twins possessed short whiskers on angular cheeks and square jaws. They were taller than Cupid and far more arrogant. They were bullies and were often referred to as lions by the other gods.

Cupid was secretly jealous of their masculine beauty.

"Mother sent us to tell you she would do it herself," Phobos said.

"Do what herself?" Cupid asked as the dread spread further through his veins.

Deimos laughed and turned to Phobos. "He can't be as dumb as he looks."

"I beg to differ," Phobos said. "He *can* be that dumb."

"Stop your antics and tell me what Mother plans to do," Cupid insisted.

"She's going to kill Ellie Beaufort," Deimos said.

"Tonight, I think," Phobos added.

Psyche flew from the front door to meet them. Her face was flushed with anger. "How can you two be so callous? That woman is innocent."

Phobos crossed his arms. "I'd like to see *you* try to stop Aphrodite."

Deimos clapped his brother on the back. "Now that would be a show worth watching."

"A short one, I'm afraid," Phobos said with a grin.

"Go on, you two!" Psyche scolded. "You've delivered your message. Now, be off!"

Once Phobos and Deimos had vanished, Psyche threw her silky brown arms around Cupid. "We have to do something, my love. We can't let your mother get away with this."

Cupid searched his wife's emerald eyes. "What would you suggest we do?"

"We have to get to Ellie before your mother does."

"Where do we start? I have no idea where the girl is."

Psyche bit her lip. Then her eyes brightened. "We could ask Hecate to perform a location spell."

Cupid wasn't thrilled about having to ask the goddess of witches for a favor, but maybe if he offered to tell her who'd been spying on her, she'd agree.

"And then what?" he asked.

Psyche shrugged. "I guess we'll cross that bridge when we get there."

Ellie stepped into her white summer dress and sandals before glossing her full lips. In her mind, she was complaining to Shalynn for making her feel like she had to keep an eye on Andrew. If it wasn't her mother wanting her to babysit Jonivan back home, it was Shalynn wanting her to babysit Andrew here.

"I ain't a damn babysitter," she said to her reflection in her bathroom mirror.

Nevertheless, she texted Shalynn and Andrew that she would be at Landon's Flats at ten o'clock. Somehow, since she never seemed to have a life of her own, she always got pulled in to doing things for other people. Not for the first time, she regretted saying she would go tonight.

She combed her fingers through her thick, curly hair, happy with the way it looked pulled back from her face. It would be a shame to stay home when her hair looked so good. Taking another deep breath, she reminded herself that she could do this. She could go for a little while—an hour, at least.

She stuffed a few dollars, her ID, her phone, her earbuds, and her dorm key into her palm-sized purse, which she wore from a thin leather strap over one shoulder. Then she took the elevator to the bottom floor to walk the two blocks to Landon's Flats.

Once she passed the main entrance to campus, she followed the road through a residential block, where it was dark and quiet. She had walked this path with Shalynn and others from the team the few times they'd convinced her to go out, but this was the first time she'd walked it alone. Now she wished she had accepted Andrew's offer of a ride. The quiet street gave her the creeps.

She pulled out her earbuds and stuck them into her ears, so she could listen to Juicy Jenkins sing, "Everything will be all right."

When Ellie reached the end of the block, she felt relieved at the sight of cars coming and going and of other people on the sidewalk in front of cafés and restaurants. The bright streetlights made it possible to see Landon's Flats all the way down on the opposite corner.

Ellie's uneasiness returned when a black sedan slowed on the street alongside her. Its dark tinted windows obscured the view inside. After a few minutes, Ellie turned into the safety of the nearest café and waited for the sedan to drive off.

Back on the sidewalk, Ellie continued in the direction of Landon's Flats, when a gust of wind lifted her hair and dress, nearly blowing her into the street. Then a bolt of lightning and a crack of thunder shot from the sky and struck the streetlight in front of her.

Ellie screamed.

A heavy sheet of rain drenched her where she stood in shock on the sidewalk.

A voice beside her shouted, "Get in!"

She turned to see Andrew in his red sportscar on the road beside her. Another guy sat in the passenger seat. The back was empty. She opened the door and climbed in.

"You okay?" Andrew asked. "That was close."

Ellie nodded, unable to find her tongue. Rain dripped from her hair and face. She was soaked.

"This is Gabe," Andrew said.

Gabe turned in the seat and gave her a grin. "It's nice to meet you. Sorry I don't have a towel on me."

The streetlight that had been struck leaned ominously over them as a blue flame sizzled and died.

"Just take me home," Ellie said.

"Yours or mine?" Gabe said with a chuckle.

Ellie wasn't amused. "Mine."

When he could, Andrew made a u-turn and headed back to campus.

"We'll wait while you change," Andrew said. "No problem."

Ellie felt like the universe was telling her to stay home. "That's okay. I think I'm done."

"What?" Gabe turned again in his seat. "You can't be done. Nothing's even started yet."

She didn't want to disappoint anyone, and Gabe was cute. He had wavy black hair that fell across his brown eyes, and he had dimples when he smiled. "I don't know."

Andrew pulled up in front of her dormitory. The rain had stopped as suddenly as it had begun.

"I'll walk you up," Gabe said, jumping out of the passenger side and opening her door.

"You don't have to," she said, but she took his offered hand, anyway.

"I know, but it'll give me another minute to try and change your mind."

She laughed as she climbed out, dripping. She could only imagine what her hair looked like plastered against her head and neck. Gabe kept ahold of her hand as they followed the sidewalk to her building.

"You probably get this a lot, but I'm a fan," he said.

"Thanks," she said. "You play?"

"In high school, but not anymore. I don't know how you do it. I barely keep up with my grades, and I don't have to worry about practice and games and all that extra pressure. It must be hard."

"It keeps me busy." She flashed him a smile. It was nice to be admired for how hard she worked.

"You have such a pretty smile," he said.

They both laughed awkwardly.

"I'm serious," he said. "I've been wanting to meet you for a while now. I was so stoked when Andrew told me he knew you."

"Good ol' Andrew," she said, not knowing what else to say.

"Please change your mind and go out with us tonight," he said as they entered the lobby of her building. "We could shoot pool, see if you're as good with a stick as you are with a bat."

That did sound fun, Ellie thought. She shrugged as they entered the elevator. She pushed the button for the third floor.

When the doors closed, Gabe suddenly took her in his arms.

"What are you doing?" she asked with a laugh. She smelled alcohol on his breath.

"I've been imagining this moment for a while now, Ellie. Please let me have a kiss."

She pressed her hands against his chest. "I'm soaking wet."

"And sexy as hell."

"Gabe, we just met."

"But I feel like I've known you for a long time." He pulled her in and tried to kiss her.

"You're crazy. Stop." She tried to act playful, laughing it off, but she was getting scared.

She was relieved when the elevator doors opened, and another student was waiting for it in the hall.

"Hey, Ellie," the girl said.

"Hey," Ellie said, pulling away from Gabe as she exited the elevator. To Gabe she said, "Well, goodnight."

"I'll walk you to your door," he said.

"That's not necessary," she said.

"I don't mind."

Gabe followed her into the hall, and when the elevator doors closed, they were alone again.

Ellie pulled out her phone and quickly texted Andrew, "9-1-1."

"Who are you texting?"

"Andrew. I'm telling him to come get your ass." She laughed, to play it off.

He laughed too. "A good wingman knows when he's not wanted."

Ellie worried she was overreacting. Most girls probably responded differently to Gabe's advances.

"I'm sorry," she said. "It's nothing against you."

Gabe took her hand. "I understand." He kissed the inside of her palm. Then he licked it, slowly.

Ellie tried to hide her disgust. "You go on without me, Gabe. Why don't we try this another time? I'm not feeling it tonight."

"That lightning almost got you. It might be a sign that you need to live each day to the fullest. You know what I'm saying?" He gave her a suggestive smile.

"Or maybe the universe is telling me to stay home tonight."

He pulled her into his arms. "Come on. Go out with me. Get to know me."

"Let's do it another time." She continued to press against his chest, as he held her close.

"Then the least I could do is tuck you into bed. Where's your room?"

She was afraid to tell him--though he could easily find out on his own. "This way."

When she pulled away from him, he grabbed her wrist and held onto her tight as he followed her down the hall. He let go of her when she stopped in front of her unit.

She took her time taking the key from her purse and inserting it into the door. As she opened it, she said, "Wait out here. I'll change and go back with you."

"Why can't I wait inside?"

"The place is a mess."

"I don't care about that." He pushed the door open and followed her inside.

CHAPTER THREE

Interventions

At the gates of Mount Olympus, Cupid said, "Spring, Summer, Winter, Fall, open the gates so that Psyche and I can enter."

The clouds lifted, and the gates parted. Cupid and Psyche flew past the stables and garage, across the courtyard, past the whale fountain, and up the rainbow steps to the main hall.

The door to Hephaestus's forge near the entrance was open. As he passed it, Cupid glanced in at the god bent over, hammering a shield. Across from the forge, Hestia could be seen in the dining room setting out a feast on the long banquet table.

In the main hall, Zeus and Hera sat together on their double throne laughing at something Hermes had said. They waved at Cupid as he and Psyche flew across the great hall and knocked on the door to Demeter's rooms.

Demeter opened the door. "Hello."

The goddess of the harvest had long yellow hair, the color of corn, and dark brown eyes, just like her daughter. But even though she was beautiful, like all the goddesses, Demeter seemed to always wear a scowl. The sulky expression diminished her beauty, in Cupid's opinion.

"Hello, Demeter," Cupid said. "Is Hecate here?"

Over Demeter's shoulder, he saw a head of long hair with black and white streaks running through it: Hecate's hair. Beyond Hecate sat Persephone with a handful of cards.

Hecate turned to face him. A smile crossed her face. "It's about time."

Demeter stepped back to allow them inside.

"I don't know what you mean," Cupid said.

Hecate's Doberman climbed from her haunches to stand beside her mistress.

"You haven't come to apologize?" Hecate asked with lifted brows.

Psyche gave him a confused glance. "Apologize for what?"

Cupid couldn't stop his cheeks from turning red. "I came to ask for a favor in exchange for information."

Hecate clicked her tongue. "How very ballsy of you to come seeking a favor after what you did."

"What did you do?" Psyche asked.

"Nothing. I was just doing my job."

Hecate clicked her tongue again. "Your job concerns mortals, not the likes of me. How's Pegasus?"

Cupid's mouth fell open. "If you knew, then why…"

"I knew you'd come when you were ready," Hecate replied.

Persephone giggled.

"What are you talking about?" Demeter asked.

"I shot you two eons ago," Cupid said to Hecate, ignoring Demeter. "I'm just trying to understand…"

"Stop," the goddess of magic replied. "Stay out of my affairs."

"Shot whom?" Demeter asked.

"We don't have time for this," Psyche said. "An innocent young woman is in danger of being killed by Aphrodite, and we need your help."

"What?" Persephone cried.

"Why didn't you say so?" Hecate scolded. "What can I do?"

"You call this messy?" Gabe teased as he stepped inside Ellie's dorm.

"I'll be right back." Ellie rushed through the living room to her bedroom.

Gabe followed her and slipped inside before she could shut him out.

"You need to wait out there while I change," she demanded without smiling.

He laughed. "The way that dress is clinging to your every curve, I think you're gonna need my help peeling it off."

"Seriously," she said. "I'm not feeling it."

"I'm feeling it enough for the both of us." He gave the bulge between his legs a squeeze as he grinned. "Check it out. You done primed the pump just by standing there, looking so good."

When he bent to grab the hem of her skirt, she kneed him in the nose. "Back off."

His hands went to his face as he groaned and stumbled back. "What's the matter with you? Bitch! That hurt! Damn! Am I bleeding?"

"No, you ain't bleeding. Now leave before I call the cops."

Ellie heard someone shouting her name. It was Andrew.

"In here!" she cried.

Andrew burst through the door and then stopped in his tracks. "What's going on?"

"Everything's fine," Gabe said. "We'll meet you at the car in a minute."

"Don't go, Andrew," Ellie said. "Not without your friend. He doesn't understand that no means no."

"You okay, Ellie?" Andrew crossed the room, putting himself between her and Gabe.

Tears filled her eyes. "Just go, okay?"

"Come on," Andrew said to Gabe.

"You go on ahead, man," Gabe insisted. "Ellie and I aren't done yet."

"Man, she said…"

"She's just playing hard to get, aren't you Ellie?"

Andrew put an arm across Gabe's shoulder. "Let's go."

Gabe lunged back and shoved Andrew toward the door. "Keep your hands off me!"

Andrew regained his balance and pushed back. Gabe threw Andrew against the wall, knocking over a lamp.

Ellie grabbed a softball from her duffle bag and threw it at Gabe's head.

Gabe fell to the floor, out cold.

Andrew's eyes widened as he looked from Gabe to Ellie.

Ellie burst into tears.

"It's going to be okay," Andrew said as he rushed to Gabe and felt for a pulse on his neck. "He ain't dead."

A crack of thunder pounded against the bedroom windowpane, causing Ellie to jump at least a foot into the air. The room filled with a blinding light.

"Andrew?" Ellie cried, unable to see her own hands.

Cupid stood in the doorway behind Psyche, watching Ellie sleep.

"What are we going to tell her when she wakes up?" Psyche asked.

Cupid took his wife's hand. "I've created an illusion. She'll think she's in her own bed, in her own room."

"And when she tries to leave?"

Cupid shrugged. "It was the best I could do."

"Poor girl."

"We won't keep her here forever. Just until Aphrodite has forgotten about her."

Psyche frowned. "That could take years."

Cupid kissed the nape of Psyche's neck and whispered, "I hope not."

"Maybe we should tell her where she is, why she's here," Psyche said.

"That would only frighten her. Let the illusion comfort her for as long as it can, or, until we figure out what to do next."

Together, they stepped from the room and closed the door.

As they turned down the hall to the west wing of their house, Cupid added, "She'll be safe here, at least."

"As long as Hecate keeps her promise," Psyche said. "Do you trust she won't tell anyone?"

"She and Hermes are close. It's possible she might tell him. And Demeter and Persephone know what we're up to as well. This could easily blow up in our faces."

Psyche led Cupid to their couch and, as they sat together, she said, "Thank you for doing this for me, my love."

"You were mortal once," Cupid said. "I think that helps you to value human life more than the rest of us, which is a good thing. We often forget that we are meant to serve humankind, and not the other way around."

Psyche leaned in for a kiss. It didn't take Cupid long to lose himself in her arms.

Ellie awoke with a start. She'd been dreaming the most bizarre dream of flying across the night sky in the arms of a red dragon. A beautiful fairy, with dark skin like Ellie's, flew beside them, occasionally stroking Ellie's cheek.

The fairy had said, "You're safe now, Ellie."

Ellie climbed out of bed and found she was still wearing the white dress from the night before, though it was dry, as was she. She felt the sheet on the bed. It was dry, too, but how could that be? She'd been soaked, and she couldn't recall drying off. The last thing she remembered was knocking out Gabe with her softball.

What had happened next? She couldn't remember Andrew and Gabe leaving her dorm room.

She searched for her phone. It wasn't on the nightstand, where she usually left it. She found her palm-sized purse draped over her desk. Her money and ID were in there, but not her phone.

She scanned the floor, checked under her bed.

"Where's my damn phone?" she muttered, on the verge of panic.

She felt all around the covers in her bed and found it beneath her pillow.

"Dang, it's dead."

She plugged it into her charger and, as soon as she could, she checked for messages.

Nothing.

She called Andrew. When he didn't answer, she texted him, "Call me asap."

Then she remembered she had class.

"Oh, shit."

It was already 10 a.m. Her class had started thirty minutes ago. She teetered for a moment with indecision, until she'd convinced herself it was better to skip than to be late.

She took a shower and changed into a clean t-shirt and pair of shorts. When an hour had passed, and she still hadn't heard from Andrew, she texted him again: "Seriously. Call me!"

Not wanting to risk running into classmates who might ask her why she wasn't in class, Ellie decided against going to the cafeteria and, instead, ate the mac n cheese she'd put in the fridge on Monday. All afternoon, she tried calling and texting Andrew. She even tried calling Shalynn but got no answer from her, either.

Around four o'clock, she decided she would go to Andrew's to find out what had happened. She slipped on her sneakers, grabbed her key, and headed down the hall.

Something looked unfamiliar about the hallway. Had she turned the wrong direction? She backtracked to her door. No. Maybe she'd just been turned around.

As she headed back toward the elevator again, she took a closer look at her phone. The time read 9:00 p.m.

"What's wrong with this phone?" She turned it off and turned it back on. This time it read 9:01 p.m.

She went to the window down the hall and saw nothing but darkness outside.

Clutching her head, she wondered if the boys had slipped her a drug last night. Either that, or she was losing her mind. She returned to her room and lay down in her bed, waiting for Andrew and Shalynn to call.

"It won't be long before she figures it out," Psyche told Cupid from where she sat beside him on the couch.

They were watching Ellie in their fireplace. Whenever Cupid shot one of his arrows into the logs stacked in their hearth, the logs would become engulfed in flames that revealed whatever Cupid desired to see. This gift only worked on mortals. Cupid couldn't use it to spy on gods.

"Look at her," Psyche said. "She's scared and confused."

"We'll tell her the truth," Cupid said. "But we should do it gradually, so we don't scare her to death."

"Ah, there she is," a male voice interrupted from behind them.

Cupid turned to see his brothers, Phobos and Deimos, standing behind the couch staring at Ellie in the flames. Phobos held the helm of invisibility, which belonged to the lord of the Underworld.

Cupid exchanged a worried glance with Psyche as he jumped to his feet. "How…"

"Our mother made a deal with Hades," Phobos explained.

Deimos chuckled. "It seems he likes having others in his debt."

Psyche stood beside her husband. "But why…"

"Aphrodite knows someone interfered with her plans to kill Ellie Beaufort," Phobos said.

"That's why she bargained for the helm," Deimos added.

Phobos pointed a finger at Cupid. "You were her prime suspect."

Psyche fell to her knees. "Please. Look at her. She's innocent."

As his brothers stared at Ellie's image in the fire, Cupid shot off two arrows. They flew directly into the hearts of Phobos and Deimos.

None but those with the blood of Eros could see Cupid's arrows, but the twins knew exactly what their brother had done. There could be no other explanation for the sudden flood of love and desire for Ellie Beaufort that flowed through their veins. Cupid could sense it. He could feel their longing.

"Brother?" Phobos clutched his chest. "What have you done?"

"I had no choice," Cupid said, full of regret. A bad situation just got worse. "This way, you'll do everything in your power to keep her safe."

Deimos narrowed his eyes. "Where is she?"

Cupid held up his hands. "Wait just a minute. The last thing you want to do is make her hate you. Am I right?"

Phobos and Deimos exchanged solemn glances before saying, "Right."

Psyche jumped to her feet. "I have an idea."

Tabby Cats

Ellie lay in bed, trying to call everyone she knew. Not a single person answered—not even her mother, who should be home at 9:30 at night. And not a single contact had replied to her texts.

Full of frustration, she slapped the phone against her pillow. "What the fuck is wrong with this phone?"

She nearly jumped to the ceiling when she heard a knock at the door to the unit. Who would be knocking at this hour? Hoping it was Andrew, she crossed through the living room and put her eye to the peephole.

There was no one there.

She pulled the door open and was about to run down the hall when she nearly stepped on a tray that had been left on the carpet outside her door. On the tray was a covered dish.

"What the…?"

As she scooped up the tray, an orange tabby cat darted into her dorm.

"Hey!" she said in surprise.

Ellie set the tray on the coffee table, and, as she was about to follow the cat to her bedroom, a second orange tabby ran into the dorm and jumped into her arms.

"Well, my goodness!" Ellie cried with surprise and glee. "Where did you come from?"

She held the cat as she shut the door to the unit—lest a third cat run inside—and then went looking for the other tabby that had gone into her bedroom.

"Here, kitty, kitty."

She found it curled on her bed beside her pillow.

Ellie laughed. "Well, make yourself comfortable, why don't you?"

The cat in her arms purred and nuzzled against her breast.

"You aren't wearing a collar," she said. "Are you strays? Or do you belong to someone? You look too healthy to be strays."

She sat on the bed next to the one tabby while she held the other in her lap. The cats purred as she stroked their fur. They had nearly identical "M" marks on their foreheads, but one had a small patch of white fur on its left hindfoot. Maybe she could take them to a vet to see if they had chips identifying their owner.

"Are you hungry?" she asked them. "I am. Let's go see what we have to eat."

She scooped up the second kitty and carried them both to the living room, where she sat on the couch. As soon as she had placed the cats on either side of her, one jumped back into her lap, which caused the other one to hiss.

"No fighting," she said, moving the one from her lap to the couch again.

She lifted the cover from the dish and was surprised to find roast, potatoes, and carrots smothered in gravy. "This looks and smells amazing. Who in the world left it here for me?"

She wondered if it might have been her coach, who'd said she would check on Ellie over the break.

Deciding that she had her answer, Ellie enjoyed her meal, offering bites to the kitties, too. But they were more interested in licking her than in eating.

"Silly kitties," she said before kissing each of their heads.

When she'd finished the meal, she carried the cats back to her room and cuddled with them in her bed.

"I'm so worried about Andrew," she told them. "That guy Gabe was horrible. I wish I knew what happened to them."

One cat licked her cheek and nuzzled her ear. The other licked her neck.

"I wish I could keep you, kitties. You're both so cute and sweet."

For the first time in a long while, Ellie didn't feel lonely. Although she still worried about Andrew and her phone, she decided she would look for Andrew tomorrow after class and take her phone to the tech shop to have it fixed. Meanwhile, she plugged the phone back into its charger, turned off the lamp, and snuggled under the blanket with the tabbies.

Cupid sat beside Psyche on their couch before the fire. They'd been watching Ellie's reaction to the cats.

"You're brilliant." Cupid kissed his wife's cheek.

"I'm glad I was right." Psyche shifted in his arms. "The twins don't fill her with fear and panic as long as they're in this other form."

"It looks like everybody's happy."

"For now. You know it can't last."

"Let's enjoy the happy moments while we can."

As Cupid held his lover in his arms and stroked her silky hair, he couldn't help but worry. Aphrodite would soon notice that the twins were missing, along with the helm of invisibility. How long before she came looking for them? And what answer would Cupid give her when she did?

"I should check on Pegasus," Cupid said after a while. "To make sure Hecate kept her word."

Psyche gave him another kiss. "Tell him I said hello."

"I need to make my rounds with the others, too," he said, referring to the horses belonging to the gods on Mount Olympus.

"I'll come for you if anything changes," Psyche assured him.

Ellie yawned, reluctant to leave the wonderful dream she'd been having. In the dream, she was being ravished by two hot men. They were identical twin gingers with hard abs and pecs and beautiful crystal blue eyes. They'd licked her breasts—she was sure she must have moaned out loud. And then they'd licked her between the legs, and she'd begged for more.

She stretched with her eyes closed, still feeling the sensation of their tongues on her body.

Then she realized her t-shirt was curled up to her neck, and the cats were licking her.

She jumped from the bed, feeling ashamed.

The tabbies looked up at her innocently from the bed.

"Silly kitties," she said, laughing it off. "I'm not your mama. There ain't no milk in here."

Suddenly remembering she had Freshman Comp, she cried, "Shit, what time is it?"

She checked her phone only to find it dead. "Ah! This fucking phone!"

Ellie stripped off her clothes and climbed into fresh ones. In the bathroom, she combed her hair with her fingers until it looked presentable, brushed her teeth, rubbed deodorant under her arms, and glossed her lips. Then she searched the unit for her sandals. Finding them, she slipped them on, grabbed her key and backpack, and headed for the door.

Then she remembered the cats. Where would they relieve themselves? She didn't want her dorm to stink.

"Come on, kitty kitties," she called. "You need to go outside."

When she opened the door of her unit, she saw what she could only believe was a hallucination. Instead of the hall to her dormitory, she was faced with an elegant corridor alight with fancy sconces that illuminated oil paintings in gilded frames. On the opposite wall were old-fashioned arched windows with lattice frames. A crystal chandelier cast sparkly images along the ceiling and walls. The carpet was replaced with shiny white marble streaked with silver and gold. She blinked, and the illusion vanished, replaced by her dormitory hall.

"Something's seriously wrong with me."

Ellie glanced back at the orange tabbies, who looked up at her with curiosity from the floor.

"Come on, kitty kitties," she said again as she stepped through the door.

The cats followed her to the elevator, where she pressed the down button. The button didn't light up, so she pressed it again. She noticed that none of the lights on the elevator were working.

"Is this elevator broken?" she wondered. After waiting for a few minutes with no sign of the elevator opening anytime soon, she said, "Geez. I guess we'll have to take the stairs. Come on."

The cats followed her as she turned down the hall, looking for the stairwell. She'd taken the stairs before, but something didn't feel right. The hall seemed unfamiliar. She followed it around another corner and suddenly felt lost. Where were those damn stairs?

She turned in the opposite direction and followed the hall to a corner, where she was sure the stairwell would be, but it wasn't. What the hell?

Trying to remain calm, she went to a window to look out on the campus, but a thick fog prevented her view. She turned down another hallway and started knocking on the nearest door. She had no idea who lived there, because she was turned around. When no one answered, she knocked on the next door and the next.

Ellie felt trapped in a nightmare, scared that she was losing her mind. She ran down one hall and then another, with the cats close behind her.

"Help!" she cried out and then stopped to catch her breath. "Someone, help me!"

When no one came, she sat on the floor in the middle of the hall and cried into her hands. She'd lost it. That was the only explanation. She'd gone completely and totally mad.

The orange tabbies curled up against her legs, bringing her comfort. She lifted them into her lap and cried into their fur.

"Thank goodness you're here," she said between sobs.

Although Cupid had found Pegasus in his stall fully recovered, his powers restored, the god of love hadn't been there long, tending to the other horses, when his mother appeared.

"Have you seen Deimos and Phobos?" she asked him.

"They came to my house hours ago," Cupid said. "And they left shortly after."

Aphrodite arched a brow. "Did they say anything to you about the girl?"

"Ellie Beaufort?"

His mother nodded.

"They said you were looking for her. I told them I wasn't surprised."

Aphrodite crossed her arms. "I hope my own son isn't undermining me."

"Of course not. Don't I always take your side in everything?"

His mother's hard expression softened. "Yes, my love. You do."

Just then, Psyche appeared.

"Is everything okay?" Cupid asked her.

Aphrodite's brow lifted with suspicion. "Why wouldn't it be?"

"Everything's fine," Psyche said. "Hello, Aphrodite. How are you?"

"I've been better, my dear. How are you?"

"Fine. I just wanted to see how Pegasus was feeling."

"He's good as new. Aren't you, Pegasus?" Cupid stroked the horse's back.

Pegasus, who didn't like to talk, winked.

"Was there anything else you needed?" Aphrodite asked Psyche.

"Um, no. I guess not." Psyche gave Cupid a worried glance.

"Perhaps I should come and have tea with you at your place, then?" Aphrodite suggested. "We girls should catch up. Wouldn't that be nice?"

"Um, yes!" Psyche said with a smile that was obviously forced. "That would be quite nice." Psyche gave Cupid another worried glance.

Cupid took Aphrodite's hand. "Would you mind doing it another time, Mother? I was hoping to get your opinion on another matter."

"Of course, darling," Aphrodite said. "What is it?"

"I'll be off then," Psyche said before she disappeared with a grateful smile.

Cupid distracted his mother by asking her opinion about Hecate and Hermes.

"Why do you suppose these two gods, who obviously care for one another, have remained celibate all these years?"

"I haven't given it much thought," Aphrodite admitted. "But, if I remember correctly, Hecate promised to remain true to Demeter. They were lovers, you know."

Cupid's eyes widened. He hadn't known.

"That was before you were born."

Cupid scratched his head. "Surely Demeter wouldn't want to prevent Hecate from moving on."

"Why, yes," Aphrodite said. "Demeter absolutely would. She relies on Hecate to protect Persephone in the Underworld for six months out of the year."

"I see."

That hardly seemed fair to Hecate. Cupid wanted nothing more than for gods and people to be fulfilled in love. It was an instinct he'd felt since birth. The unquenched desire between Hecate and Hermes disturbed Cupid.

"Well, if that's all you needed from me, I should go," Aphrodite said. "Your brothers are missing, along with another item of great importance."

"And what might that be?" Cupid asked, though he knew the answer.

"It's probably best you don't know," his mother replied, just before she kissed his cheek and disappeared.

Cupid god-traveled directly home, where he found Psyche standing before their hearth. The fire beneath revealed an image of Ellie sobbing into her hands with Phobos and Deimos in their cat form draped across her lap.

"It's time to tell her the truth," Psyche said.

CHAPTER FIVE

The Bright Fairy

Ellie took a deep breath and dried her eyes with the back of her hands. As she picked up the cats, one in each arm, and climbed to her feet, something strange happened: the dormitory hallway shifted back into the hallucination she'd experienced earlier.

"What the…" Ellie blinked, but the hallucination did not go away.

Her throat was suddenly dry—so dry she couldn't swallow. He heart pounded, and so did her head. She stared at the marble floor streaked with silver and gold, the chandelier hanging overhead, and the walls lined with oil paintings illuminated by fancy sconces.

"Hey, kitties?" She backed up against a wall for support—for her knees felt weak, and she thought she was going to faint. "Do you see what I see?"

She closed her eyes and opened them. The marble floors remained beneath her feet. The hallucination hadn't stopped.

"Ellie?" a voice called from around the corner.

"Coach?"

The woman who stepped into view was not her coach but the beautiful fairy from her dream. Her skin, though dark like Ellie's, glowed with an almost blinding luminosity, and her emerald eyes sparkled and were nearly as blinding as her skin.

Ellie blinked against the brightness. "Am I dreaming?"

"No, I'm afraid not," the fairy said gently. "Don't be frightened. You're perfectly safe."

That's what the fairy had said in Ellie's dream.

"There, is that better?" The fairy's luminosity dimmed.

Ellie could now see the fairy with perfect clarity. She wore a short red dress and leather sandals. Her dark hair fell in waves across her shoulders and back. Emerald eyes gleamed beneath long, dark lashes and equally dark brows. Her features were flawless, and her glowing brown skin gave her an otherworldly appearance.

Ellie clutched the cats close. "What's happening?"

"Come with me, back to your room, and I'll explain everything as best as I can."

The fairy turned and walked down the hall. Since Ellie didn't know what else to do, she followed.

When they reached the door to her unit, Ellie found it wasn't her dorm room at all. In its place, she found a large ornate suite with a queen-size canopy bed against the far wall. Trembling from fright, Ellie looked around, gaping. To the right was a fireplace with a green chenille chaise lounge angled in front of it beside a round golden ottoman. There was a dresser to the left with a basin of water, and, past that, a door to what appeared to be a bathroom as large as a spa. Ellie held the cats close and looked up. The ceilings were *coffered*—a term she had learned from watching many episodes of *House Hunters* while she dreamed of one day owning her own home, unlike her mother, who'd never escaped government housing.

The dark coffered ceiling, with its enormous crystal chandelier, had an intricate design where each beam crossed. The intricate design was repeated in the dark wood trim around the fireplace and in the gold and brown rug in the middle of the marble floor. The gold in the rug was the same gold on the walls and their elaborate moldings, and it appeared to be *actual* gold—not just in color.

Ellie looked around, gaping, for many seconds. What had happened to her dorm?

"As you might have guessed, you're no longer at your school in America," the fairy said gently.

"What? I'm in a different country?" Ellie could hardly breathe.

"Yes, you are. But the point is, you're safe."

"But how did I get here?" She blinked again and again, expecting to wake up from a dream.

"My husband and I brought you, to protect you."

"To protect me from what? Where am I? What is this place?"

"My home," the fairy said. "My husband and I live here, on a hilltop in Greece. Won't you have a seat?"

The fairy motioned toward the chaise lounge. The cats leaped from Ellie's arms and took a seat on the green chenille by the cozy fire. Ellie, still in a daze, joined them, unable to hide her trembling.

"My name is Psyche," the fairy said. "My husband's name is Eros—though everyone calls him Cupid."

Ellie gave a nervous laugh. "You're kidding, right?"

"I know this is a lot to take in. I can remember what it was like for me, though it was so very long ago."

"What are you talking about? What's going on?"

"I was once brought here by the red dragon, too. I was taken from my friends and family because I was in danger."

There'd been a red dragon in Ellie's dream. Had the dragon saved Ellie from Gabe? Or was Ellie still dreaming? "What danger?"

Psyche sat on the golden ottoman across from her. "Have you heard of Aphrodite?"

"I don't know much about Greek mythology, but I've heard of *her*."

"Mythology?" Psyche frowned. "You're not a believer, I gather."

"Can you just tell me what's going on?"

Ellie still wasn't convinced that she hadn't lost her mind. Maybe she was lying somewhere in the hallway, passed out, experiencing a crazy delusion. Or maybe she'd already been admitted to a psychiatric ward, and this fairy was a doctor or a nurse, and Ellie's crazy brain was distorting everything. Or maybe Gabe had slipped her a drug and everything since then had been one massive trip.

"Am I tripping out?" Ellie asked. She'd never used drugs before. This must be what they did to you.

"You see that portrait above the mantle?" Psyche gave a nod toward the fireplace.

The portrait was of a beautiful woman with sparkling blue eyes and long, golden curls that tumbled down white shoulders. Her features were impeccable.

"That's Aphrodite," Psyche said. "My mother-in-law."

Ellie decided it was useless to argue. "And what does she have to do with anything?"

Both cats stopped licking her lap and looked up at her.

"What's the matter, kitties?" she asked them.

They returned to their licking.

"Are they bothering you?" Psyche asked.

"They're the only things that *aren't* bothering me," Ellie said.

Psyche sucked in her lips and nodded.

Ellie realized she'd offended the fairy—or whatever she was.

"I'm sorry," Ellie said. "I think you're trying to help me. Aren't you?"

"Yes, I am. You see, well, there's no gentle way of saying this. Aphrodite is jealous of you and wants you dead."

Cupid sat on the couch before the fireplace, watching what the flames revealed to him. Psyche was doing her best to answer Ellie's questions, but the girl continued to be afraid.

"You aren't a prisoner here," Psyche was saying, her voice carrying through the flames. "More like a refugee, under our protection. You're free to roam the castle, so long as you have someone with you. The cats will protect you."

"The cats?"

"These aren't ordinary tabbies. You don't need to feed them or to worry about a litter box," Psyche explained. "They're special cats—your guardians while you're here."

"And how long will that be?" Ellie asked.

"I don't know. For as long as is necessary to keep you alive."

Cupid was surprised when one of the cats leaped from Ellie's lap.

Ellie's voice held a hint of desperation when she said, "Where are you going, kitty?"

"I'm sure he'll be back," Psyche reassured her.

Moments later, Phobos appeared in Cupid's living room. Although his red hair was a shade darker than the orange of his tabby fur, his crystal blue eyes remained the same, and they were smoldering.

"This situation isn't ideal," Phobos said.

Cupid could feel the unquenched desire flowing through Phobos, through the arrow still in his heart. "Give it time."

Phobos cocked his head to one side. "How much time?"

"It's only been a little over a day. More time than that, brother."

"I may be the cat's meow," Phobos began, "but there's only so much a cat can do for a woman."

"I understand. I'll introduce you."

"When?"

Cupid had never seen his brother try harder to hide his desperation. "Soon. I swear it."

Phobos sighed. "I must admit, it feels nice to bring a mortal comfort, instead of fear, for once."

"Don't get soft on me, brother." Cupid grinned.

"I never said I was purr-fect."

Cupid shook his head and clapped his comedian of a brother on the shoulder. "I'll invite her to dinner, so she can meet you—and Deimos, of course."

"Do we have to include him?"

"I'm afraid so." Then Cupid said, "I will find a way to undo what I've done to you. I promise."

"Undo it to Deimos, but not to me," Phobos said. "I've never felt more alive than I have these past few hours."

"Because you've never loved before, but you could again. You could love a goddess and have an eternity of happiness."

"I want Ellie."

"Of course, you do." Cupid realized it was useless to argue with him.

"I'll never forgive you if you take this feeling away from me, brother," Phobos said. "And that is no joke."

Phobos disappeared, leaving Cupid unsettled.

Relieved when the second orange tabby returned to her lap from wherever he had gone, Ellie turned to Psyche. "Are you the one who left the roast and vegetables for me last night?"

"That was my husband. Would you like to meet him?"

"I don't know. Does anyone else live here?"

"Just my husband and I…and the cats."

A man poked his head through the door. He appeared to be the same age as the fairy—maybe mid-twenties—and had the same golden curls and crystal blue eyes as the woman in the portrait over the mantle.

"May I come in?" the man asked.

Ellie's mouth fell open as she turned back to Psyche.

"That's my husband, Cupid," Psyche said. "He helped me save you. There's no need to fear him."

The man looked nothing like a winged cherub.

"What happened?" Ellie asked the man named Cupid in the doorway. "The night you came? What happened to the guys who were with me?"

Cupid scratched his head. "I'm afraid I was too busy dodging my mother's attempts to kill you with her father's lightning bolts to notice the other mortals."

Ellie frowned. "Oh."

"But I can find out," Cupid added. "Would you like that?"

"Yes, but what I'd really like is to go home—back to my dorm, I mean."

"It isn't safe," Cupid said.

"I'd rather take my chances," Ellie said. "No offense, but I don't know you. How do I know you're telling me the truth? You say I'm not a prisoner here. If that's true, then let me go back."

The fairy leaned forward and took Ellie's hands. "We will. I promise. Eventually. But, please, stay for a little while—long enough for us to distract Aphrodite."

"You can have anything you want while you're here," Cupid said. "Your every wish is our command. We can serve you your favorite foods, show you your favorite films, provide you with your favorite books."

"And I can bring you beautiful gowns, like you've never seen!" Psyche squeezed Ellie's hands. "And jewels!"

"And the best music," Cupid said. "And art."

"Can I have internet?" Ellie asked.

Psyche let go of her hands and sighed.

Cupid chuckled. "What is it with mortals and their internet?"

"It helps us to feel connected," Ellie explained. "So, can I have it?"

"As long as you don't interact with others," Cupid said. "You can read all you want, but, for your own safety, you mustn't post anything."

Yeah, right, Cupid, Ellie said in her mind. *I'm contacting everyone I know as soon as possible to get me the hell out of here.* "Okay. Where's my phone?"

Cupid pulled it from his pocket and handed it to her. "There's no need to charge it. You can access the internet, but you won't be able to call or text or post anything."

Ellie looked it over. Her phone seemed to be working, though it didn't show any missed calls or texts. Later, she'd try to call her coach. "Can I play my games and listen to my music?"

"As often as you like," Cupid said. "And why don't you plan to eat your dinners in the dining room from now on, instead of staying locked up in your room?"

"Do I have to?" Ellie asked. "I kind of like being alone, with the cats."

"My brothers want to meet you," Cupid said. "I've asked them to come for dinner tonight. Eat wherever you want whenever you want, but tonight I'd like you to join us."

Why would his brothers want to meet *her*? Why did *any* of them care about her?

Ellie took a deep breath and nodded—still not sure if everything that was transpiring was anything more than a strange delusion. She supposed she should play along until things returned to normal.

"There's a closet through that door." Psyche pointed toward the spa-like bathroom. "You'll find plenty of things to wear."

"Do I need to dress up for this? Or can I wear jeans?" Ellie asked.

Psyche turned to Cupid. "Shouldn't we go all out for our first dinner together?"

"Plan to wear a gown," Cupid said. "My brothers will be wearing their finest, and we wouldn't want them to feel overdressed."

Ellie nodded again. "How much time do I have before dinner? And how will I know where to go?"

Psyche pointed to a grandfather clock in the corner of the room. "It's Greenwich Mean Time here, nearly noon. You may be feeling a little off because it's still evening back where you came from."

Ellie studied the clock. She wasn't used to reading Roman numerals. It took her a few seconds to understand that it was 11:45. Her phone displayed the same time, thank goodness.

"We should give her some lunch," Cupid said. "Most mortals eat three times a day. She's probably hungry."

Although her stomach growled, Ellie didn't think she could eat. She felt numb and was still in shock over all that was happening. "I'm okay. But what time is dinner?"

"Seven," Psyche said. "To get to the dining room, take a left in the hall, go down the stairs, and cross through the grand foyer."

"You can't miss it," Cupid added. "Meanwhile, feel free to explore the castle, but don't go out into the garden without one of us."

That was the first thing Ellie wanted to do—after calling her coach. She wanted to get outside and run.

CHAPTER SIX

Escape

When they were alone together, making their way to their bedroom, Psyche said to Cupid, "Why are we having dinner with your brothers? Are you sure that's a good idea?"

"Phobos came to me while you were talking to Ellie. He's losing his patience. The dinner is my way of pacifying him."

"You know how they'll affect Ellie, in their godly form—even dimmed."

"Yes, I know."

His brothers would fill an already terrified girl with mortal fear and panic.

Psyche shrugged. "I suppose they have to meet sooner or later. Let's just hope she's ready for this."

"She's not," Cupid said. "But I don't think we have much of a choice."

After they reached their bed chambers, Cupid kicked off his shoes and stripped out of his clothes. Because he worked in the stables each day, he took frequent baths. Psyche usually joined him. Bathing was one of their favorite things to do together.

He was pleased when Psyche began to undress, too.

"I wish I could know her thoughts," Psyche said as she tossed her red dress on the bed.

"Ellie didn't know it, but she prayed to me back there. She told me that she was going to try to contact everyone she knew for help." He went to their bathing pool and felt the water with a toe. "Mmm." It was hot—just the way he liked it.

Psyche followed. "Well, of course she doesn't trust us…*yet*. She will in time."

"I hope you're right, or it will mean misery for us all."

Cupid gazed over his wife's naked body. It was as beautiful and as inviting as it had been the day that he fell in love with her. He stepped into the hot water and took her hand. She followed him into the pool.

The first thing Ellie did when the mysterious man and woman named Cupid and Psyche left her was search through her contacts for her coach. Finding her coach's number, she clicked on it and prayed the call would go through. It didn't. Next, she tried her mother and got the same result. She phoned Shalynn. Still no connection. She threw her phone across the room onto the queen-size canopy bed and groaned.

The kitties nuzzled against her, bringing her comfort as tears spilled into her eyes. She crossed the room to the bed, took up her phone, and clicked on her Facebook app. When her status didn't post, she tried instant messenger. When that didn't go through, she tried Instagram. She went through every social media channel she could think of, including email, but none of her posts or messages would go through.

"I've got to get out of here," she said to the cats, who had jumped onto the bed.

One of the tabbies cocked his head to the side.

"You can come with me, if you want," she said, tucking her phone in the back pocket of her shorts. "You might be special guardian cats, but, if you want to fly the coop, come on."

The cats hopped from the bed and followed her from the room. She had been told she could explore the castle, so there was no need to be sneaky, she reminded herself, as she stepped into the hallway.

The castle was quiet as she turned left and padded down the hall, noticing the oil paintings of beautiful people on her left and gorgeous arched windows with crisscross lattice on her right. When she peered through one of the windows, she saw the angled rooftop of the first floor below.

The hall ended with a curved stairwell, mirrored by another on the opposite end of a long balcony to her right, with an enormous heart-shaped window looking over the first-floor rooftop.

The ceiling was coffered with dark beams and the same intricate design as the ceiling in her room—except this ceiling was much higher with an even larger crystal chandelier hanging over the grand foyer. The double staircase, with its dark wood railing, formed a heart, like the enormous window behind it. A red carpet ran the length of both sets of stairs.

Ellie descended the stairs with the cats on her heels. The front door was at least seven feet tall, made of dark wood in the shape of an arch. Should she run through it or leave through a back way?

When she reached the foot of the stairs, she peered in the opposite direction of the front door, through a wide cased opening leading to a banquet table.

"The dining room," Ellie whispered.

She strolled around the long ornate table and the twenty or so high-back wooden chairs, as though she were taking a self-guided tour, in case anyone was watching her. She walked past a gilded mirror hung over a curvy side table with drawers and cabinets, to a set of double French doors. Through the windowpanes, Ellie saw a kitchen, and there was someone—or something—standing at the stove.

Ellie covered her mouth to stifle her gasp as she turned and crept away. It had been a satyr!

She left the dining room, crossed through the foyer beneath the crystal chandelier, and headed for the front door. She expected it to be locked, but when she turned the large golden knob, the tall, heavy door opened inward. As quickly as she could, Ellie slipped out, with the two cats following.

Ellie's instinct was to run as hard and as fast as she could. She hurdled over flower beds and neatly trimmed shrubs, past statuary and a golden sun dial. When she came upon a sparkling stream, she ran alongside it, down the slope of the hill, both frightened and exhilarated, with the cats on her heels.

She hadn't realized how high above sea level the castle was. The further she got from it, the steeper and rockier the slope became. And although she could now see for miles and miles—both land and ocean—her view was occasionally obstructed by clouds, reminding her of the few times she'd flown on an airplane.

"This is a damn mountaintop," she muttered, wondering how on earth the man and woman had gotten her there. Had they flown her by plane? Helicopter? There didn't seem to be any roads. For the first time since she'd ran from the castle, she worried she might not make it down. There were some scary, steep parts ahead of her.

Daunted by how far she would have to climb to get to the base of the mountain, she kept running alongside the stream for as long as she could, even though the air seemed thin and cold, and her heart pounded faster than usual. The cats kept pace with her. She was comforted by their presence.

Fortunately, the sky was clear, so, except for the chill in the air, she wouldn't have to battle the weather. Maybe if she got far enough down, she'd find an outpost, or possibly another human being. Maybe a plane or a helicopter would fly by and notice her. She tried not to give up hope, even though the real danger of falling to her death was slowly beginning to sink in.

After some time, Ellie came to a stop, panting in the chilly breeze. She'd already passed these same boulders, this same part of the stream. She glanced back at the castle a few hundred yards away at the top of the peak and realized what she'd done.

"We've been running in a circle," she said to the cats, who had stopped beside her. "I guess we'll have to cross the stream if we're going to make it down."

She gazed across the water to the opposite bank. It was about fifty meters away.

"I wonder how deep it is."

Carefully, because of the rocks, Ellie walked out into the cold rushing water. She'd only gone a few steps when she said, "Coming, kitties?"

She turned back in time to see two men, identical twins—young and built and ginger, like the guys in her dream. One of them rushed to her—seemed to fly, even—and swept her up in his arms, holding a finger to her lips.

"Ssh," he whispered.

Too frightened to speak, she stared back at him, dumbly.

She felt a brief pressure followed by a blinding light, and, the next thing she knew, they were beside the boulders, and he was helping her to climb inside the dark space between them—a kind of cave.

"Hide," he whispered.

He pulled her onto his lap, and, when she searched his face for some clue as to what was going on, he put his finger to his lips and then to hers, to silence her.

The touch of his finger to her lips aroused her despite the mortal fear pumping through her veins. His crystal blue eyes promised protection even though his very presence paralyzed her.

His musky scent, his hard body, and the sheer size of him took her breath away. He possessed a rugged beauty with a formidable jaw and brows and penetrating eyes. She could get lost in those eyes.

He pointed up, where she heard footsteps.

"Hello, Mother."

Ellie turned toward the sound of the voice. Through the crack between the rocks, she saw the other twin, though he was brighter than the one who was holding her. The brighter twin stood before an equally bright woman.

Ellie gawked. It was the woman in the painting over the mantle in her room—the woman Psyche had said was Aphrodite.

"Hello, Deimos. Where have you been? Why haven't you answered my prayers?" the woman said.

The tall ginger put his hands on his slender hips. "I've been busy doing as you asked. I told you I'd tell you when I had any news."

"Where's Phobos? And the helm?" Aphrodite crossed her arms.

"Phobos is wearing the helm while he spies on Cupid."

"And why aren't you with him? What are you doing out here?"

"I thought I sensed something, but I was mistaken. Maybe it was *your* presence I felt."

"Has there been no sign of Ellie Beaufort?"

At the sound of her name, Ellie gasped. Her protector cupped his hand to her trembling lips.

"I'm afraid not. And no lead—yet. But we aren't convinced that Cupid doesn't know something. Just give us more time."

"I want that girl found," Aphrodite insisted. "She's all the mortals are talking about. It's worse than it was before! Now that she's gone missing, they can think of nothing else! I want them to see her dead body, so we can put an end to this!"

Ellie felt a scream rising in her throat. She pressed her protector's hand harder against her mouth, which, to her surprise, made him grin.

"I'll report back to you as soon as I know something," Deimos said.

"Thank you, darling," Aphrodite said. "And thank your brother for me—Phobos, I mean. I still can't believe Cupid would turn on me."

"We don't know that he has," Deimos said.

"Good for you, for keeping an open mind," his mother said before she kissed his cheek and vanished into thin air.

Ellie's eyes widened, and the scream that had been rising from her chest escaped, though it was muffled by the hand belonging to her protector.

"You're safe now," he said. "Don't be afraid."

Ellie wanted to say, "Easier said than done." She wanted to say anything, but she could only stare back dumbly at the man who had protected her.

"It's safe to climb out," he said to her, still grinning, but now with a new kind of arrogance. "Unless you want to remain on my lap."

Heat rushed to her cheeks, and she averted her eyes. With trembling legs, she climbed from the tiny cave, expecting to find the other twin. Instead, one of the tabbies jumped into her arms and licked her chin.

She immediately felt better. "Hello, kitty. Where's your friend?"

From behind her, her protector said, "I'll see you tonight, Ellie."

She turned, hoping to thank him, now that she'd found her tongue, but he'd disappeared. The other tabby brushed his fur against her leg and purred.

"There you are," she said, relieved he hadn't run away.

She kissed the cat in her arms before setting him down beside his friend. Then she stroked the other one and kissed him, too.

Whether all that was happening was part of a drug-induced trip, a psychotic breakdown, or a dream from which she hadn't been able to wake, Ellie decided to begin the steep hike back toward the castle. She and the cats stepped over rocks with no clear path to follow. It would be a lot slower going up than it had been coming down.

It seemed to Ellie that the best course of action was to behave as though what was happening to her was real. This way, if by some strange chance she *had* been abducted by gods wanting to protect her from being killed by another god, then she'd be better off cooperating. Also, if it was all a delusion, she'd be no worse off for acting as if it weren't.

But, if it *were* all true, then what Aphrodite had said about everyone looking for Ellie back home would also be true. Was Ellie's mother worried? Her coach? Her teammates?

"Good," Ellie said out loud. Maybe they would appreciate her more.

So, her captors were real, she told herself. From now on, that's what she would believe. They were gods named Cupid and Psyche. They'd saved her from being killed by Aphrodite and were keeping her in their castle until Aphrodite was no longer a threat. They'd given her two special guardian cats to keep her company, and they'd offered to give her anything else she wanted in the form of food, books, music, art, film, clothing, and jewels. Why shouldn't Ellie make the best of it? Even if this were a delusion, why fight it?

The best part about this strange experience so far had been sitting on the lap of the most beautiful man she'd ever seen, feeling his hand against her lips as she gazed into his deep blue eyes. He'd grinned when she'd pressed his hand harder against her mouth. He'd even teased her about wanting to stay on his lap.

Wait, he'd also said he would see her later tonight.

Was he one of the brothers of her captor, who would be dining with her that evening?

Ellie's mouth fell open as she continued her hike. The ginger twins were Deimos and Phobos, and the one who'd been holding her was Phobos. Cupid had said his brothers wanted to meet her. Ellie smiled and bit her bottom lip.

"Why would Deimos and Phobos want to meet *me*?" she asked the cats.

They rubbed up against her legs and walked beside her in silence.

Whatever their reasons for wanting to meet her, she couldn't wait to meet them. Having decided to resign herself to this crazy delusion, she was excited to spend some time with the sexiest men she'd ever seen. She picked up her pace, anxious to return to the castle to have a bath and to find something beautiful to wear. No longer focused on escape,

Ellie wanted nothing more than to impress the two brothers who had saved her.

As she neared the castle, she was struck, for the first time, by its magnificence. Made of golden bricks, it was rectangular with four towers, each topped by a spire. Three levels had rows of arched windows. The arch was repeated in the massive front door, covered by a portico that bore a flag with the same intricate detail Ellie had seen on the coffered ceilings. In its larger form, Ellie recognized the image. It was a crest depicting two birds with their beaks and breasts touching, forming the shape of a heart.

A beautiful garden filled with fruit trees and flowering shrubs surrounded the castle. Flowering vines climbed trellises, and roses bloomed near the door. Ellie admired the white-stone statuary of goddesses and nymphs around a fountain. Then she remembered the satyr in the kitchen and stopped in her tracks.

The cats circled her legs and looked up at her.

Ellie reminded herself that she was going to believe in this delusion and that she was going to trust that the castle was safe—even if a satyr lived in it.

She walked into the grand foyer, where she was greeted by Psyche.

"Did you enjoy your time in the garden?" the goddess asked.

Ellie laughed, not sure if "enjoy" was the right word to describe her experience. She'd been terrified, running for her life; yet, she'd felt exhilarated, too. Likewise, sitting on Phobos's lap had been both terrifying and exhilarating.

"Yes," Ellie said. "Thank you."

"I heard about your close call," Psyche said. "I hope you'll be more careful in the future."

Blushing, Ellie nodded. "News travels fast."

"You have no idea."

Ellie wasn't sure what to say to that.

"And you met my brothers-in-law, Phobos and Deimos?" Psyche asked.

"Just Phobos," Ellie said, unable to stop a smile from cracking her face in half.

Psyche's brows lifted in surprise. "He didn't frighten you?"

"He saved me. He *and* his brother, Deimos. I didn't get to meet *him*, but I saw him."

One of the cats leapt into Ellie's arms.

"Interesting," Psyche said. "Well, there's food in the kitchen, if you can't wait until dinner."

"No, thanks. I can wait." Ellie would rather avoid the kitchen. "I think I'll go have a bath and figure out what I'm going to wear tonight, if that's okay."

"Of course." Psyche smiled, apparently pleased. "Call me if you need help."

"Thanks." Ellie carried the one tabby in her arms and was followed by the other across the grand foyer to the stairs, but she'd only taken a few steps when she turned back to Psyche. "How do I call you?"

"Just say my name," the goddess said. "You don't even have to utter it out loud. You can pray to me, and I'll hear you."

"You can hear my prayers?"

"Only when you direct them to me," Psyche said.

"Oh." To test it, Ellie prayed, *Psyche, you have beautiful eyes.*

"Thank you," Psyche said. "I think your eyes are lovely, too."

"Whoa," Ellie said. "Okay, that was freaky."

"If you need anything, just wish for it," Psyche said. "But still feel free to pray to me if you need my help."

Ellie thanked the goddess and continued her ascent toward the heart-shaped window on the second floor before she turned down the hall toward her suite. The door was open, as she'd left it. She closed the door behind her and stroked the cat in her arms.

"Might as well make the most of it," she told herself again.

CHAPTER SEVEN

Bathing with Cats

Ellie set the orange tabby down on the rug inside her suite beside the other and locked the door. Grabbing her phone from her back pocket, she said, "Okay, Google. Play 'Not Today,' by Juicy Jenkins."

When the music played through her phone, she said to the cats, "Juicy Jenkins is so lit. This is one of her best. It's too bad we don't have a blue-tooth speaker, so we can hear it better."

Just then, a movement in her peripheral vision caught her eye. She turned to find a blue-tooth speaker on the nightstand beside the canopy bed. It hadn't been there before.

"What the…"

She looked at the kitties on the floor by her feet, "Did you guys see that?"

One of them cocked his head to the side. The other licked his paw.

Ellie synced her phone to the speaker, and "Not Today" blasted through the room.

"Well, all right!" Ellie laughed. "Now we just need a disco ball!"

A flash of light nearly blinded her. She closed her eyes and opened them to find that the crystal chandelier had been replaced by a glitzy disco ball.

Whether she was delirious from all the crazy that had been happening to her, or giddy from having just met the sexiest man alive—whose eyes and touch she couldn't get out of her mind—Ellie began to dance and sing. The cats pranced around the room with her, delighting her. When the song ended, she fell back on the canopy bed and laughed with glee. The cats hopped up beside her and licked her face as she giggled and stroked their fur.

"Okay, Google," Ellie said. "Play 'Take it Off,' by Juicy Jenkins."

Once the music began again, Ellie jumped up to dance and sing, this time performing a strip tease for the kitties.

"Take it off!" she sang. "Just take it off!"

"I'd prefer you didn't watch this part," Psyche said to Cupid from where she sat beside him on the couch.

Cupid grinned. "Jealous?"

"What if I am?"

"You sound like Aphrodite."

Psyche pouted.

Cupid took her silky hair and wound it around his finger. "I'm teasing you, Beautiful. I wouldn't want you to take pleasure in another's body, either."

"There's no other body I prefer to yours," she said with invitation in her eyes.

He closed the distance between them. "Nor I yours," he said against her lips.

Ellie tossed her t-shirt onto one of the tabbies and laughed when he got stuck inside of it. She tossed her shorts onto the other tabby, who picked them up in his mouth and carried them around the room.

"Where are you going with those?" she teased.

She helped the cat that was caught in her shirt to freedom but then tormented him further by taking off her bra and strapping it around him.

Then she jumped around, singing "Take it off," feeling free and alive, which was ironic. For all she knew, she had died and gone to heaven.

As the song came to an end, she pushed her panties down and stepped out of them. Then, turning her back to the cats, she bent over, put her hands on her knees, and shook her bottom.

Then she hopped around with her arms in the air singing, "Ta-daa! Did you like that, kitties?"

The cats looked up at her and purred.

Cupid left his wife in charge at home, so he could tend to his duties among mortals. It would be irresponsible of him to deny the pleasure that true love brings to those who were suffering in agony, longing for a partner to make them feel complete. Some couples were easier than others to bring together. Some needed only a casual meeting on a bus or a train. Others required years of strategic moves, painful heartbreaks, and other significant endeavors—sometimes even loss or betrayal—to get the couple to the right place to fall in love.

The prayers to Cupid were never-ending. He couldn't know it for certain, but he suspected that, of all the gods, only Thanatos received more prayers than Cupid. People prayed for love, and they prayed to be spared from death, or they prayed for those things on behalf of their loved ones.

Often, his mother worked with him to orchestrate the best partnerships, but she put him off again today because of her obsession with Ellie Beaufort. Cupid wished he could convince Ares to abandon whatever scheme he was planning with Apollo and Tiresias to take Aphrodite to Paris for a few months.

But even if his mother *could* be made to forget about Ellie, the same could not be said of his brothers. Because of their duties, neither god had had the opportunity to fall in love. Ares relied on the gods of panic and fear to help him wage wars. Artemis used them to keep hunters and their prey properly balanced. Athena used them to deter crime and carry out punishment. Even the Furies of hell needed them to help torment the evildoers sentenced to Tartarus.

Cupid had been forbidden by both his mother and father to shoot his arrows into the hearts of any of his siblings, save Harmonia, because their duties required their complete devotion. So even if Cupid's protection of Ellie could be kept a secret forever, it wouldn't take long for his parents to discover that something was different about their twin sons.

But the worst problem of all was the fact that Cupid had bound the hearts of his brothers to a mortal—someone who would eventually die and leave them heartbroken for the rest of eternity. Never had Cupid wished more desperately for a way to undo the power of his arrows. And although he loved his wife and wanted to please her in all ways, he regretted putting the life of the mortal before the well-being and happiness of his brothers.

If his brothers were mortal, Cupid could borrow two arrows of hate from his aunt Eris and use them to neutralize his arrows of love. But arrows of hate were forbidden from use on gods, because the arrows could drive them to commit abominable acts against the innocent.

For the moment, Phobos and Deimos were happier than they'd ever been, full of the sweet bliss of pure romantic love and desire. It didn't matter that the object of those feelings hadn't also been shot by Cupid. To do so, he would have had to choose one brother over the other, and, since he loved them equally, such a choice was impossible. But it didn't matter, because Ellie was essentially their prisoner and had no choice but to entertain their company. And if she rejected them as men, well, they had already won her heart as cats.

Phobos and Deimos were having the time of their lives, but, when the time came, would they be able to forgive Cupid for what he had done to them?

Ellie fell on the canopy bed, laughing. The cats jumped on top of her—one on her stomach and the other on her lap. She removed her bra from the one tabby and asked, "Better?"

They purred and licked her skin, sending shivers of delight across her body.

"You two cuties," she said, stroking them. Then she covered her eyes. "I think it's time we lose the disco ball."

When she opened her eyes again, the disco ball had vanished, and the crystal chandelier had returned.

"That is so dope," she said.

Then she sat up, causing the one tabby to hop from her stomach to the bed.

"Let's take a bath," she said. "I need to get ready for tonight. I want to make a good impression on Phobos and Deimos. Come on!"

The cats followed her to the bathroom—which looked more like a spa with an indoor pool. The pool was in the shape of a square and was surrounded by marble steps. A marble swan stood in the center with water flowing from its beak. Ellie leaned over and moved her fingers through the water. It was surprisingly hot—but not too hot.

"Oh, that's nice," she said.

She looked around the room for soap and shampoo and found them near a golden sink. Then, taking the bottles with her, she climbed into the hot pool. It was the perfect depth. She lay with her head resting on the marble ledge. If she hadn't been so excited about the dinner with Cupid's brothers, she could have easily fallen asleep.

She was surprised when the orange tabbies followed her into the water.

"It's not too hot for you, kitties?"

They paddled to her side and climbed onto her breasts. Their warm bodies comforted her, and she lay there, sighing, completely content.

But after a few minute's rest, she sat up and shampooed her hair. She rubbed some of the shampoo into the fur of the cats and gave them a bath, too.

"Does that feel good?" she asked as she rubbed their backs and scratched them behind the ears.

For the first time, she noticed that their eyes were crystal blue.

"You have such pretty eyes, kitties."

She laughed when one of them hit the water with his paws and splashed her in the face.

"Did you do that on purpose?" she teased as she wiped the water from her eyes.

Once they were all rinsed and scrubbed clean, Ellie climbed out and searched for towels. Finding them, she dried herself and then each of the cats. She laughed when they shook out their fur, sending drops of water in all directions.

"It's time to decide what to wear."

With a towel wrapped around her hair like a turban, she walked naked across the marble floor to the enormous walk-in closet. Three rows of clothing hung neatly from the racks, and shelves lined with shoes took up an entire wall.

"Are these my size?" she wondered as she picked up a gorgeous boot.

To her surprise, they were. She picked up one shoe after another, finding every single one to be her size.

Could the same be true of the gowns, dresses, suits, and slacks?

The kitties hopped onto the bench in the middle of the closet to watch her pick through the garments. Every item of clothing was exactly her size. Ellie had never seen such beautiful clothes and couldn't believe they were all at her disposal to wear whenever she wished.

An hour had passed by the time she'd narrowed the evening's options down to three gowns. She tried them each on, modeling for the kitties, who seemed to approve.

One was a satin emerald dress with a high neck and a low back and a high-low hem—short in the front with a trail in back. The hem in front barely reached the top of her knees, and the dress hugged her hips and thighs like a glove. The dress was sleeveless and flattering, but the low back was too low, revealing the top of her crack.

"I wonder if this dress would get a rise out of Phobos," she said to her reflection in the mirror.

One of the cats stood up on his hind legs and briefly pawed the air, as if he were batting a fly. The other cat, the one with the white left hindfoot, hissed.

"That's enough," she said to the one who'd hissed.

She stepped out of the gown and returned it to the rack.

Before putting on the second gown, she removed the towel from her head and used her fingers to comb her curls and get them in place while her hair continued to dry. She found two golden barrettes and used them to hold her hair back from her face.

Happy with the result, she climbed into the cream-colored gown covered in lace. Unlike the emerald gown, this one had a skirt and bodice. The bodice was a low v-neck, showing plenty of cleavage, with buttons in the back. Ellie managed to button a few—enough to see how the dress fit. The skirt was full and touched the floor. The sleeves were long, ending in a point on the top of each hand. Now that she saw how it looked on, Ellie thought the gown resembled a wedding dress, which wasn't the look she was going for.

"Next," she said, as she unbuttoned the few buttons she had reached.

She returned the dress to its hanger and pulled out the lavender gown. The silk felt nice as she stepped into the dress and zipped it in back. The color made her skin glow, and, like the emerald one, the gown hugged her like a glove. It had a scooped neckline in the front and back, capped sleeves, and a slit on one side that reached the top of her thigh.

She liked that it didn't show as much cleavage as the cream gown, but that it still showed enough to make her feel sexy.

"I think this is the one," she said to the kitties. "What do you think?"

The kitties looked up at her and purred.

"Now to find the right shoes," she said as she searched through the dozens of pairs.

She pulled out a silver, glittery pair of stiletto heels and sat on the bench between the tabbies to slip the shoes on. They fit her beautifully.

"Let's see if I can walk in them."

She climbed to her feet and took a few steps.

"They ain't like my running shoes, that's for sure."

She took a few more steps. "This will take some effort, but I don't care. I aim to *amaze*."

CHAPTER EIGHT

The Helm of Invisibility

Ellie sat at the vanity in the spa-like bathroom of her suite experimenting with the makeup she'd discovered in a drawer. She rarely wore makeup, but the few times she had, she'd received lots of compliments. Since she was inexperienced, she watched a few Youtube tutorials to get ideas. By six o'clock, she had done everything she could think of to make her hair, face, and body look as radiant as possible.

"Well, kitties, we have an hour to kill before dinner. It can't get here soon enough."

She practiced walking in the heels, catching glimpses of herself in the three-way mirror of the enormous closet and feeling horrified at her profile.

"These heels are making me slouch and look stupid."

She tried pulling her shoulders back and lifting her chin, but she only looked more ridiculous.

"Just great." She kicked off the shoes and checked out her reflection as she walked barefoot. "That's better. Now I don't look so dumb." She turned to the cats. "But I really liked those sparkly shoes. Let's see if there's another pair I like. I really want to make a good impression tonight."

As Ellie picked through the other dozens of shoes, she said, "I don't know why I care so damn much about making a good impression. What do I know about these guys, anyway? I mean, I'm grateful that they want to protect me from their crazy mother, but that doesn't mean I should throw myself at them, right, kitties?"

The cats looked up at her and then at one another.

"For all I know, they could be jerks, just like…other guys I've met." She didn't want to think about Gabe, because it made her feel slimy and gross.

"Why do I even want to go to this stupid dinner?" Her stomach hurt, from not having had anything to eat all day. "Maybe I'll just tell them I don't feel good. It's true. All of a sudden, I *don't* feel good."

One of the cats rubbed his head against Ellie's ankle and then pressed his flank against her, wrapping himself around her leg.

"If I don't go, that means I can spend more time with you sweet things." She picked up the tabby and kissed him on the head before setting him back down again.

As if he were jealous, the other cat came and rubbed his head against her other leg. She picked him up and kissed him, too.

"You kitties always make me feel so much better. I'm going to that dinner, and I'm going to make the best of it."

She set the second kitty down and returned to the wall of shoes, rummaging through the dozens of pairs.

"Ah, here we go."

She found a silver pair of open-toed shoes with an ankle strap and a short wedge. She buckled them on, walked around, and then said, "So much better."

But she still had forty-five minutes to kill.

"I can't stand it anymore. I'm just going to explore the castle until dinner. Want to come, kitties?"

She was surprised when they didn't follow her. Weren't they supposed to be her special cat guardians?

"Suit yourselves," she said as she headed out the door.

Instead of going toward the double stairs and the grand foyer, Ellie went to the right, toward the back of the castle. She glanced through the arched windows, with their crisscross lattice, to the angled rooftop be-low and spotted a black owl with gray eyes. It looked up at Ellie before it flew away.

To Ellie's right, between the golden moldings on the walls, were por-traits, illuminated by sconces, and these portraits appeared to be of other gods and goddesses. She came upon one of Cupid and another of Psy-che. Further down, she saw a goddess with a shield, bow, and arrow. Past that were Phobos and Deimos—she wasn't sure which was which. She studied their portraits, noting any differences. They both had dark brows and vibrant red hair that brought out the crystal blue of their eyes. But one parted his hair in the middle and the other on the side. The one with the side part also had a slightly longer nose and slightly thicker lips—though the mouths of both men were equally luscious.

Thinking back to her protector, who'd held her in his lap, she re-called that he wore his hair parted on the side. People change hairstyles all the time, so there was still no way of knowing which portrait was of which twin.

She continued her stroll down the hall. Because her suite was so large, she had to walk quite a way before she came upon another door, and it was ajar.

Full of curiosity, Ellie slowly pushed the door open—ever so slight-ly—and peered inside. It was a bedroom suite, not unlike hers, with a fireplace, canopy bed, and sitting area—though this one also had a desk and a different color rug and bedding. The coffered ceiling was identical to the one in her room, but the chandelier was iron rather than crystal, and the mantle on the fireplace was different, as was the portrait hang-ing above it.

She stepped inside to see if there was also a spa-like bathroom. Standing in the doorway in nothing but a towel wrapped around his waist was one of the ginger twins. His hair was wet but combed, and it was parted in the middle.

Ellie covered her mouth, unable to find the words to speak. Along with her feeling of embarrassment for her intrusion was another one of panic. Adrenaline surged through her. Her heartrate dramatically increased. She felt as if she needed to fight or flee.

"Hello," the ginger god said with a wide grin. "You must be Ellie."

"I'm so sorry," she finally managed to mutter. "I didn't mean to walk in on you like this."

"No need to apologize. You look lovely, by the way."

"Oh, thank you. You look…" her cheeks burned as she glanced back toward the door. She wanted to run. "I'll just go."

She hustled from the room as fast as the glove-like dress allowed her.

Continuing down the hall, she muttered, "Ellie, you idiot." Then she paused near her bedroom door, which she had left open, to catch her breath and pull herself together. Once her heartrate had returned to normal, she proceeded toward the grand foyer.

Standing beneath the chandelier was the other twin, clean-shaven and dressed in a tuxedo. As soon as she saw him, she knew who he was, and, just like before, he took her breath away.

"Phobos," she said, as she reached the bottom step.

As she neared him, she was overwhelmed with fear.

"Hello, again," he said with a twinkle in his eyes. "I see you're early, too. Whatever shall we do for, let's see," he looked at a watch on his wrist, "twenty minutes?"

She stared at him with wide eyes. She felt paralyzed and helpless.

He cocked his head to the side, reminding her of one of the kitties. "Cupid may or may not have explained to you that I'm the god of fear. What you're feeling right now…that's simply a byproduct of being near me. There's not *actually* any reason to be afraid."

She understood what he was saying, but it didn't change the way she felt. She stood frozen. Her heart felt as if it had stopped, and she could barely breathe.

"Maybe it would help if I told you a joke," he said suddenly. "Someone once told me I was one of the top five funniest persons in the entire world—which I'd say is a high compliment considering the fact that there must be at least thirty-seven."

"Ugh," she managed to say.

"See?" He laughed. "It's working."

Ellie took a deep breath, trying to calm herself down.

"Something else I'm told," Phobos said with a grin. "I'm so good at sleeping that I can do it with my eyes closed."

Although she still couldn't move, Ellie snorted.

Phobos threw his head back and guffawed. "That one gets them every time."

"You're bad," Ellie teased.

"That's another thing people say about me, though they aren't usually referring to my sense of humor."

Ellie lifted her chin. "What are they referring to, then?"

Phobos gave her wink. "I'm all kinds of bad, sweetheart."

"Especially at jokes."

"Well, I know a lot of jokes about the unemployed, but none of them work."

"Stop. Please!"

He offered her his hand. "Only if you let me escort you to the dining room."

When she put her hand in his, the paralyzing fear surged through her all over again, but she reminded herself to take deep breaths, and she managed to follow Phobos, the god of fear, across the grand foyer, through the wide cased opening, and into the dining room.

"You look incredible," Phobos said under his breath as they reached the long banquet table.

"So do you," Ellie said, without meeting his eyes.

But a moment later, she had another shock: the satyr walked in from the kitchen and began setting the table. Ellie clutched Phobos's arm and gasped.

"For once I'm not the scariest thing in the room," Phobos said with a grin.

The satyr rolled his eyes at the god and muttered, "Very funny."

Phobos turned to Ellie. "See? I told you everyone here finds me hilarious."

Ellie laughed. "Okay, okay. You win."

"Do you hear that, Deacon?" Phobos said with a chuckle. "I win." Then he turned to Ellie and whispered, "Just so you know, I always do."

His warm breath on her skin made her shiver with pleasure. She wanted so badly to think of a clever comeback, but all she could do was smile at him and remind herself to breathe.

"You're early," Deacon said. "Can you come back in five minutes? I should have everything ready for you by then."

"It looks like we're being kicked out," Phobos said to Ellie.

"What should we do?" she asked.

"I know just the thing," he whispered. "Come with me."

He took her hand again, sending another shock of paralyzing fear through her body.

"Think happy thoughts," he said, when he noticed her hesitation.

She focused on his amazing good looks and charm and on his corny sense of humor, and these reminders helped her to put one foot in front of the other. Phobos led her into a library, a room at the front of the castle off the grand foyer.

"Do you read?" he asked as he crossed the room to a golden chest with a chain around it.

"On and off," she said. "I go through phases. My longest reading phase happened in the sixth grade. I was obsessed with the *Warrior* series. Have you heard of it?"

He shook his head.

"It was a very long series about cat warriors," she said with a laugh.

Phobos grinned. "Are you a cat lover?"

"My mom is allergic, so I could never have one growing up. I didn't have *any* pets, and I was always jealous of my friends who did. I adore the two cats in the castle and hope I can convince Cupid and Psyche to let me keep them when I leave here."

"You never know," he said as he unchained the golden chest. "You might just get your wish."

"Do you really think so?" She hadn't believed it could be a real possibility.

Phobos shrugged. "It wouldn't hurt to ask."

"I will then." She missed the kitties and wished they had come downstairs with her.

"I'm about to show you one of the most important objects in the entire world." Phobos lifted the lid of the chest and frowned. "It's…"

"Here." Deimos appeared beside her as he removed a helmet from his head. He wore a black tux that was nearly identical to his brother's.

Ellie flinched and squealed at his sudden appearance. Then adrenaline pumped through her, and she couldn't decide whether she should fight for her life or flee.

"Think happy thoughts," Phobos reminded her. "This is Deimos, the god of panic. Brother, you aren't helping our problem by startling her like that."

"Sorry," Deimos said. "For once, you're probably right."

"How long have you been spying on us?" Phobos asked.

"Brother!" Deimos said with mock offense. "How dare you accuse me of such a violation of privacy and trust?"

"How long?" Phobos asked again.

"I walked in during the discussion of the cat books," Deimos said.

Phobos moved his lips close to Ellie's ear, sending shivers of pleasure down her spine. "I'm not sure we can believe him."

"I have excellent hearing, you know," Deimos teased. Then he turned to Ellie and took her hand. "It's nice to meet you with clothes on."

Phobos cocked his head to the side. "What did I miss?"

Deimos grinned. "Nothing much. Just Ellie walking in on me after I had my shower."

Phobos clenched his jaw and rolled his eyes.

Ellie was enjoying the boys' banter, and Deimos seemed to take her smile as a sign that she was on his side, because, still holding her hand, he led her from the room as he said, "My brother was right about this being one of the most important objects in the world. It's called the helm of invisibility, and it belongs to Hades, lord of the Underworld."

She glanced back at Phobos, who followed, wearing a sullen expression.

Deimos held her hand as he returned the black iron helm to his head. Then he held a finger to his lips—in the same way Phobos had done earlier as they hid beneath the boulders.

"Very funny, Deimos," Phobos said. "How very predictable of you."

Deimos mouthed, "He can't see us."

Still holding her hand, Deimos led Ellie to a mirror in the grand foyer and pointed.

"I can hear her shoes striking the marble floor," Phobos said as he followed.

Ellie gasped when she could see neither Deimos nor herself reflected in the mirror. She could only see the reflection of Phobos, who stood a few feet behind them. Deimos removed the helm, and their reflections appeared in the mirror, with Phobos behind them.

"That's crazy!" Ellie cried. "How does it work?"

"Only the Fates know," Phobos said.

"But," Deimos began, "we do know that whoever wears the helm can protect those he touches."

"That's why I was invisible, too?" Ellie asked.

"Exactly," Deimos said. "You see, after Zeus and his siblings overthrew their father, Cronus, the Fates gave a powerful gift to each of the three brothers. Zeus received a lightning bolt, Poseidon a trident, and Hades this helm."

"I always wondered why the sisters didn't get a gift," Phobos said. "Pretty sexist, don't you think?"

Ellie chuckled. "Is it wise to criticize the Fates? They must be very powerful if they're capable of giving away such incredible objects."

"Very powerful, indeed," Deimos said. "As are their gifts. The lightning bolt and trident will easily kill a mortal and paralyze a god."

"Can the helm kill or paralyze anyone?" Ellie asked.

Deimos shook his head.

"Sounds like Hades got the raw end of that deal," Ellie said.

"Not really." Phobos snatched the helm away from his brother. "Some might say he got the best gift of the three."

"For once, I agree with my brother," Deimos said. "Gods are usually swift enough to elude an attack from the bolt or the trident. It's also important to understand that, while gods can easily make themselves invisible to mortals, only the helm makes them invisible to one another."

"Now, that's enough lessons for today, brother. Let's go eat." Phobos disappeared and then reappeared without the helm. "Ready?"

Each god offered her his arm, so she took them and allowed both twins to escort her to the dining room. She noticed, as she walked between them, that having them on either side of her seemed to neutralize the effects they each had on her, making her neither paralyzed with fear nor pumping with the need to fight or flee.

Cupid stood near the head of the table to greet his guests as they arrived. Psyche was already seated at his right, looking radiant, as always, in a gown of midnight blue chiffon. Cupid was delighted to see his brothers and his mortal guest smiling. Perhaps this arrangement wasn't going to be so miserable, after all.

However, Cupid was concerned that his brothers had shown Ellie where they'd hidden the helm. Worried that their desire to please her was clouding their judgment, he decided he'd speak with them privately later.

He pulled the chair to his left from beneath the table and offered it to Ellie. Phobos took the seat beside her, and Deimos sat beside Psyche across from his brother.

"You look lovely," Psyche said to Ellie as the mortal took her seat.

"Thank you," Ellie said. "That means a lot, coming from someone as beautiful as you."

As Cupid settled back into his chair, he was relieved that Ellie seemed to know how to appease a goddess.

"Deacon," he called. "We're ready for our first course."

CHAPTER NINE

Dining with Gods

Ellie had stiffened with fear the moment Deimos had left her side. The satyr's entrance from the kitchen hadn't helped her predicament.

Phobos murmured in her ear, "Think happy thoughts."

His warm breath on her cheek sent a shiver down her neck.

"She seemed fine when you first walked in," Psyche said. "Is their presence too fearsome for you, Ellie?"

Ellie waited for the satyr to finish serving her soup. Then she said, "I can handle it." To the satyr she said, "Thank you."

"You have excellent manners," Cupid said.

Deimos nodded. "Megaera would approve."

"Megaera?" Ellie asked before taking a sip of her soup, which was creamy and delicious and not like any soup she'd ever eaten.

"She's one of the Furies," Deimos explained. "She and her two sisters torment evildoers in Tartarus. Meg is especially fond of punishing those with bad manners."

"Thank you, Professor Deimos," Phobos said dryly. Then to Ellie, he added, "He has a way of creating teachable moments, so he can show off his inventory of useless information."

Deimos rolled his eyes. "Better the professor than the clown."

"Roll your eyes some more," Phobos said. "Bet you won't find a brain back there."

"Are you calling *me* an idiot?" Deimos asked his brother.

"No, that would be an insult to idiots," Phobos teased. "You just talk like one."

"Only when I need *you* to understand me."

Phobos chuckled. "Come on, Deimos. You're like Monday mornings. Nobody likes you."

"He thinks he's a smart ass," Deimos said playfully to Ellie from across the table. "But he's really just an ass."

Psyche couldn't hide her grin.

"Brothers, please," Cupid said. "Let's not argue in front of our guest."

"We want her to feel at home," Psyche said before taking a drink of her wine.

"Believe me. My sister and I are a lot worse," Ellie said. "Sibling rivalry is the only thing here that's at all like home."

Deimos and Phobos flashed her their nearly identical grins while Cupid said, "Well, I suppose that's *something*."

When Ellie had finished the delicious soup, she asked the twins, "Do you two live here, with Cupid and Psyche?" It seemed likely, because she'd walked in on Deimos dressing, but Psyche hadn't mentioned the twins when Ellie had asked who else resided in the castle.

"No. We have our own place," Phobos said.

"Together?" Ellie asked.

"Technically, we have rooms in our father's abode on Mount Olympus," Deimos explained. "But we prefer our bachelor pad in London."

Ellie wondered how many women they'd entertained in their bachelor pad, and she found herself feeling inexplicably jealous. She took a sip of her wine. "What is your father's abode like, on Mount Olympus? Is it a castle, like this one?"

"It's a temple," Deimos said, "with elaborate rooms for each of the most powerful Olympians."

"I'll take you there one day," Phobos offered. "Mount Olympus is the most beautiful place on earth."

Ellie couldn't imagine anyplace more beautiful than Cupid and Psyche's castle. "And who did you say your father was?"

"Ares," Cupid replied. "God of war."

"He keeps Phobos and me fairly close," Deimos said. "We help him manipulate conflicts, along with countless other duties."

"I'm surprised he hasn't come looking for us." Phobos drained the last of his wine from his glass.

"He has," Psyche said. "We told him we hadn't seen you since the day Ellie disappeared."

"He'll be back," Deimos said.

"You're right about that, brother," Phobos said. "It's just a matter of time."

Ellie frowned. How safe could she be if the god of war was looking for her supposed protectors?

"Deacon," Cupid called. "We're ready for the second course."

The satyr returned from the kitchen and cleared their empty bowls.

"Thank you," Ellie said when he took hers. Now that they'd made a point about her manners, the pressure was on to be extra careful with them.

"So, tell us about *your* father," Cupid suggested when Deacon had returned to the kitchen.

"I never met him," Ellie replied. "My mother was young and had a lot of boyfriends." She'd decided not to tell them the truth—that her mother had resorted to prostitution just to survive. "When she got pregnant, she decided not to tell any of them, since she couldn't be sure which one was responsible."

"Why didn't she have a paternity test?" Psyche asked.

Ellie did not like the direction their conversation had taken, but she didn't dare be rude to gods. "I wish she would have. I think it was selfish of her not to. We could have used the help and support of a father—especially since my mom did the same exact thing two years later, when my sister came along."

"Your sister doesn't know her father, either?" Deimos asked.

Ellie shook her head, feeling pathetic. She wanted to change the subject.

"We can try to find out," Phobos said. "We can try to find out the identities of both fathers, if you want us to."

"How?" Ellie asked.

The satyr entered with a tray and began to lay plates of filet mignon in front of each of them.

"I don't think that's a good idea, Phobos," Cupid said. "We have other things to worry about right now."

"That's okay," Ellie said after thanking Deacon for her plate. "I'm not sure if I want to know, anyway."

"Of course, you want to know," Deimos insisted. "Every child does."

"We can look into it after the threat on your life has passed," Phobos said. "If you want us to, that is."

Ellie had to admit, if only to herself, that she was curious. The idea of finally knowing the answer, after she'd invented so many fictitious possibilities, sounded liberating.

Phobos squeezed her hand. For a moment, she couldn't breathe.

"You okay?" Phobos asked, his face close to hers.

"Perhaps you should avoid touching her," Deimos said to Phobos. "It's paralyzing, brother."

"At least it doesn't make her want to run for her life," Phobos said. "Or punch my face."

That made Ellie laugh.

"Am I right?" Phobos laughed, too.

"But you do make it almost impossible to breathe," Ellie said to Phobos.

"It's better not to inhale when you're near him, anyway," Deimos teased.

"Don't start again," Psyche said.

"The truth is," Ellie began, "I feel best when *both* of you are touching me. I think you cancel out each other's effect on me."

Deimos stood up. "Why didn't you say so earlier? Phobos, scoot down."

Phobos groaned. "Seriously?"

"Don't you want Ellie to feel comfortable?" Deimos asked.

"It's not too much trouble to move one place down," Psyche pointed out.

Phobos looked at Cupid.

"Don't look at me," Cupid said.

Ellie was disappointed with the sullen look on Phobos's face. In her mind, she said, *Don't be a baby, Phobos.*

As if he'd heard her, he lifted his brows, and, without saying a word, got up, took his plate and glass of wine, and moved down.

Ellie followed suit.

As soon as Deimos sat beside her, she felt at ease again.

"We don't even have to be touching for me to feel the difference," she said. "Just being in the middle of you two helps."

"Glad to be of service," Deimos said with a wink.

Damn, you're cute, she thought.

Deimos patted her thigh and sent a shock of electricity through her body.

"Why don't you tell us more about yourself, Ellie?" Psyche suggested. "You play softball, isn't that right?"

Ellie had just taken a bite of the filet mignon. It was so tender, that it melted in her mouth. "Yes."

"Why softball?" Cupid asked.

Ellie shrugged. "Because I'm good at it, I guess. Playing comes naturally to me."

"How did you get started?" Deimos asked.

"We played in elementary school. My coach took me under his wing and convinced my mom to let me play in the city league."

"And she did?" Psyche asked.

"Only because my coach wouldn't leave her alone until she said yes. My mom used to see it as a waste of time, especially when I started playing select. That changed the day I got my full ride to Florida State."

"I bet you're proud," Phobos said, finally coming out of his sulking. "Good for you."

"Thanks." Ellie took one more bite and felt too full to eat anymore. "This was so good. Thank you again. I'm stuffed."

"We still have three more courses," Cupid said.

Ellie laughed. "I'll try my best."

As Deacon brought out the third course, a plate of noodles smothered in white sauce, Ellie asked the gods about their lives, hoping to get out of having to talk more about her own.

"I find it interesting that the goddess of love and beauty is married to the god of war," she said.

"They're not married," Phobos said.

"Oh," Ellie looked down at her plate and played with the noodles, chastising herself for making assumptions.

"You see," Deimos began. "Centuries ago, Aphrodite was betrayed by her own father."

Ellie asked, "And her father is?"

"Zeus," Phobos replied.

"See, Zeus's son Hephaestus was born lame," Deimos continued. "And legend has it that Hera tossed her imperfect child from Mount Olympus."

"Some people think that Hera thought her child had been stolen and replaced with a monster," Cupid said.

"Hera won't talk about it," Psyche added.

"And Hera is Zeus's wife?" Ellie asked, feeling dizzy from all the names.

"Yes," Phobos said. "Professor Deimos, do we really need so much backstory? Get to the point."

"Okay," Deimos said with a hint of annoyance in his voice. "To get back at his mother, Hephaestus designed and crafted a beautiful golden chair, which he presented to Hera as a token of forgiveness and reconciliation. But it was a trick chair. After sitting on it, Hera was stuck for days and days."

"TMI, brother," Phobos complained. "The point."

"The point is," Cupid said. "Zeus had promised our mother that she could marry her true love, our father Ares, but when Zeus saw Hera so distressed, he announced that whoever could free his wife could have his daughter's hand in marriage."

"Hephaestus freed Hera, and Aphrodite was forced to marry him," Deimos said.

"How sad," Ellie said. "For both of them."

"Exactly," Psyche said. "Everyone should be with their one true love."

Phobos and Deimos exchanged a significant look. Cupid's complexion reddened. Ellie wondered what she had missed.

"Aphrodite and Hephaestus secretly divorced centuries ago," Deimos added. "But not all the gods know and very few mortals, if any."

"Then what's stopping your parents from getting married?" Ellie asked.

Phobos gave a dry laugh. "The gods try very hard to conceal their weaknesses and mistakes from those who worship them."

Ellie had never considered the possibility that gods had weaknesses or made mistakes. She supposed they were good at hiding them. "So, you two help your father with wars..."

"That's just the half of it," Deimos said. "My brother and I are needed by most of the Olympians."

"It's true," Phobos said. "They couldn't do their jobs without us."

"And you make people afraid," she said to Phobos. "And full of panic," she said to Deimos. "Doesn't that bother you? That you're making people feel so bad?"

Cupid cleared his throat. "Mortals couldn't have achieved half of what they've accomplished without Fear and Panic. Their fear of death, for example, is what motivates people to invent modern medicine and technology. And Panic is what gives a mother the surge of adrenaline she needs to save her child from a burning house."

Deimos added, "You know that tingling sensation you get when the hair raises on the nape of your neck and your body is telling you to run?"

Ellie nodded.

"That's me saving you from a grizzly bear, or a snake, or a rapist," Deimos said.

Ellie hadn't thought of that. "You two are more important than I realized."

"Guarding you almost feels like a vacation," Phobos said with a grin.

"But if you're here protecting me," Ellie began, "others are in danger. How will they know to run from a grizzly bear without Fear and Panic?"

"Artemis can help with the wild animals," Deimos said. "And there are other gods who can intervene."

"What about you, Cupid?" Ellie asked. "Is it true what they say about you?"

Cupid laughed. "I don't know. What do they say?"

"You make people fall in love by shooting them with your arrows."

"It's a little more complicated than that," Cupid said. "Two people should be destined to be together. And they must be looking at each other, or at images of one another, when my arrows strike for the bond to form. Although I try not to, I regret that I've made some mistakes." Cupid glanced at his brothers.

"So, it *is* true," Ellie said with surprise. "Did you shoot *my* heart?"

"Why would you ask that?" Psyche asked, looking from one brother to the next.

Suddenly feeling very vulnerable to the gods on either side of her, Ellie asked herself the same question. Had she just given away her intense attraction to them?

Ellie wanted to reply, "Because I'm an idiot"; instead, she said, "I don't know. Doesn't he shoot everyone at one time or another?"

"No," Cupid said. "Not all lovers are meant to be. And not all people are meant to be lovers."

"How do you decide?" Ellie asked.

"The Fates usually decide these things," Cupid said. "And my mother and I have the ability to intuit them. We also have discretion, which the Fates honor."

Ellie was glad she was no longer the focus of their conversation. "That's fascinating," Ellie said. Then she turned to Psyche. "And what about you, if you don't mind my asking?"

"I'm the goddess of sacred unions. I work with Hera to help married couples stay together. It's not easy work, especially when Hera abandons me to rein in her own husband, who has a wandering eye."

Phobos chuckled. "He has more than a wandering *eye*."

"I hope you don't speak of your *own* father with such irreverence," came a voice behind them.

Psyche jumped to her feet. "Ares!"

Ellie covered her mouth and gazed with trepidation at the burly, red-haired god behind her.

Ares folded his bulky arms. "Why can't you boys ever do what your mother asks of you?"

CHAPTER TEN

Ares, God of War

Cupid stared up at his father, in shock. "How did you get past my wards of protection?"

"It's sad that my own son wants to prevent me from entering his house," the god of war replied.

"Not under normal circumstances," Psyche said, coming to Cupid's defense.

"We knew you'd side with Mother," Phobos said. "It's that simple."

Ares began to pace. "Nothing's that simple."

"What do you mean?" Deimos asked. "Has something happened?"

Ares walked around the table to stand behind Psyche and to study the mortal girl.

Cupid noticed that his brothers were poised to protect her, should their father strike. He was certain that their father had noticed it, too.

"I see I'm too late," Ares said.

"Too late for what?" Cupid asked.

"You shot them, didn't you?" his father accused. "You shot your brothers and bound their hearts to a mortal girl—the same mortal girl."

Cupid was aghast.

Psyche covered her mouth. "How…" Psyche's voice trailed off.

Ellie's face turned white.

Cupid struggled to form words. One of his brothers beat him to it.

"Father." Deimos stood from his chair. "Why on earth would you say such a thing?"

"Apollo knew this would happen." Ares made a fist. "He had a vision. That's why your mother wanted Ellie Beaufort dead."

Ellie gasped.

"Mother never mentioned this to me," Cupid said, feeling confused.

"She was trying to protect you," Ares explained. "She thought if you knew the prophecy, that, like King Oedipus, your attempts to avoid it would only make it true."

"Who's King Oedipus?" Ellie whispered to Deimos.

Deimos sat back down in his chair, leaned close to Ellie's ear, and murmured, "A demigod king who was warned by Apollo's oracle that he would one day kill his father and marry his mother, and, in trying to avoid that fate, Oedipus essentially made it happen."

Cupid felt a bead of sweat forming on his brow. How did Apollo's vision have anything to do with him?

"Instead, it was your mother's own interference that brought this upon us," Ares muttered. "How ironic."

"You're talking in riddles," Phobos said.

"Tell us what you know," Deimos demanded. Then he added, "Please, Father."

Ares took the seat beside Psyche, who was still on her feet.

"You better sit down," Ares said to her.

Psyche returned to her chair.

Everything seemed to be happening in slow motion. Afraid of what was to come, Cupid took his wife's hand and prepared himself for the worst.

Ellie hadn't realized she'd been holding the hands of Phobos and Deimos until she felt Phobos give her hand a reassuring squeeze. At what point had she taken them? Or had they taken hers?

She watched on in silence and with dread as they waited for the god of war to put an end to their confusion.

"About a week ago, Apollo came to me," Ares began. "He'd had a vision of disaster for the Olympians."

"What did he see?" Cupid asked.

"He said it came in bits and pieces, but he saw Mount Olympus quaking as both your brothers lay in the arms of this woman."

Ellie blanched when Ares waved a finger at her.

The twins avoided meeting her gaze as she sought each of their faces for answers. Had Cupid really shot them with his arrows and bonded both these gods to her?

Ares continued, "He saw the three of them in one bed as the pillars of the great hall came crashing down."

Ellie's face burned. Now she was the one unable to meet anyone else's gaze. She released the hands of the twins and covered her face.

"Did he say what the vision meant?" Phobos asked.

"Apollo and I went to see the Fates," Ares said. "They told us the time would come for all Olympians to learn humility."

"To learn humility?" Deimos repeated. "What does that mean?"

Ares heaved a heavy sigh. "The Fates refused to say much, but they did tell us that the gods had separated themselves too much from humanity. They said Zeus ordered the creation of mortals and all but abandoned them."

"What does that have to do with us?" Phobos asked.

"They said that Ellie Beaufort's fate was connected to the reckoning."

"What reckoning?" Cupid asked.

"Apparently, ours," his father replied. "The Olympians."

Ellie bit her lip as the gods around her seemed to process their father's message.

Ares continued, "When Apollo and I weren't satisfied with what we had learned from the Fates, we paid the old seer Tiresias a visit in Tartarus, but not before your mother had already interfered."

"Did Tiresias shed any light on this bewildering puzzle?" Deimos asked.

"He said there was nothing we could do to prevent the reckoning from coming," Ares said. "And by trying to prevent it, we would only speed up its arrival. He also said we wouldn't believe him—that no one ever does."

Ares pounded both fists on the table, upsetting a glass of wine.

The wine spilled across the table and fell onto Ellie's lap. She jumped to her feet, but not quickly enough. Her beautiful lavender dress was spoiled.

Ellie tried to resist, but she couldn't prevent herself from bursting into tears. It was all just too much.

"I'm sorry," she muttered.

Deimos touched her arm, but Ellie pulled away and ran from the room.

Cupid could sense his brothers' hearts pining for the mortal as she fled the dining room.

"I'll go," Psyche reassured them before she followed Ellie out.

"None of this makes any sense," Phobos said.

"I agree," Deimos said. "And it sounds like the reckoning is connected to Ellie, but that doesn't mean she *causes* it."

"Why did Mother involve me in the first place?" Cupid wondered out loud. "If she'd killed the girl herself, then…"

"Don't say it," Phobos said.

"You're breaking our hearts," Deimos added.

Cupid swallowed hard. "So how do we prepare for this…*reckoning?*"

Ares shrugged. "Your mother had hoped the death of the mortal would change the prophecy. It still might."

Ellie searched her rooms for the tabbies but found no sign of them.

"Ellie?"

It was Psyche standing at the door.

"May I come in?" Psyche asked.

Ellie nodded. "Have you seen the kitties?"

Psyche crossed the room and took a seat on the golden ottoman in front of the fireplace.

"Won't you please sit down?" Psyche motioned toward the green chaise lounge. "I'm sure the cats will return soon."

Ellie sat on the chaise, trying to keep the wine stain from touching anything. She'd wiped her tears, but more were on the verge of spilling from her eyes.

"I can easily help you with that," Psyche said as she waved her hand in the air.

The wine stain vanished. Ellie's gown was good as new.

"Thank you," Ellie said. "But I wasn't really crying about the dress."

"I know, dear."

"I still think I must be dreaming."

"I really wish you were," Psyche said. "But you're safe here."

"Am I? Because I'm not so sure."

"You have four gods who'll do anything to protect you."

"And yet Ares got in. What if others come—others who want me dead?"

"Ares slipped past our wards because he's the one who taught us how to make them," Psyche said. "And only he knows their vulnerabilities."

Ellie wasn't convinced.

"Besides," Psyche continued. "We have the helm. We can hide you under its protection. It's one of the most powerful objects in existence."

"Can I have it close by, just in case?"

"I'll be sure of it." Psyche stood. "Why don't you change and get some rest, and I'll see you in the morning?"

"If I live that long."

Psyche squeezed Ellie's shoulders. "You will. I'll see you then."

"Psyche?" Ellie asked.

"Yes?"

"Is it true—what Ares said about Cupid shooting his brothers? Are Phobos and Deimos really in love with me?"

Psyche returned to Ellie's side and put an arm across her shoulders. "It's true. But it's a good thing, Ellie. It's their unending love for you that will keep you alive."

Psyche crossed the room to go, but, at the door, she turned and said, "Remember, if you need my help, just pray to me. Okay?"

Ellie nodded. "Please leave the door a little open for the kitties."

Psyche pulled the door, leaving it open a crack, and disappeared.

Ellie wished she would have asked the goddess for a fire in the fireplace.

As soon as she'd wished it, a fire bloomed on the hearth.

Cupid turned to his brothers, who'd looked overcome with despair ever since their father had left. "Don't worry, brothers. With Ares on our side, Ellie is safe."

Cupid sounded more confident than he felt. Ares seemed sincere when he'd said that he wanted his sons to find happiness for as long as possible, but Cupid had known Ares to disregard their feelings before.

Phobos combed his fingers through his red hair. "His plan is pointless."

"Don't say that," Deimos said.

"Even if he could succeed in bribing Apollo and Hades to keep their mouths shut about the prophecy," Phobos began, "we have no way of preventing others from discovering it—if they haven't already."

"True," Deimos admitted. "Apollo isn't the only god with visions. What if Hecate sees it and alerts everyone on Mount Olympus?"

Psyche appeared at his side. "I have an idea."

The twins both looked at her with skepticism.

Phobos narrowed his eyes. "No more playing cats."

"But she needs those kitties," Psyche objected. "As I was leaving her, just now, she asked me to keep the door open for them."

"You have to admit, brother," Deimos began, "it's had its perks."

"Those cats can't abandon her now," Psyche said.

"I agree," Cupid said.

"Just hear me out," Psyche said.

"We're listening," Phobos said.

"One of you should guard her at all times beneath the helm," she said. "You should stay within an arm's length so that you can god-travel her away from here at the first sign of trouble."

"I volunteer," Deimos said.

"Now, wait a minute," Phobos objected.

"Let me finish," Psyche insisted.

"No more interruptions," Cupid said to his brothers. "Go ahead, Psyche. Tell us your plan."

"I know it's difficult for you to be away from Ellie," Psyche said. "So, while one of you is hidden beneath the helm, the other of you should comfort her—distract her from thoughts of her mortality— sometimes as a cat and other times as a man."

"I'll take that job," Phobos said.

"Wait a minute," Deimos argued.

"Let her finish," Cupid said.

"You should take turns," Psyche said. "Every twenty-four hours, the one beneath the helm will pass it to the other."

"Phobos can have the helm first," Deimos said.

"No." Cupid stood from his chair. "You'll draw lots."

CHAPTER ELEVEN

Deimos

Ellie found a nightgown in one of the dresser drawers and slipped it on after returning the lavender gown to the closet. As she folded back the covers on the canopy bed, she wondered for the hundredth time where the orange tabbies had gone.

Just then, the door to her room opened slightly.

She hurried toward it. "Kitties?"

"I've been called worse," Deimos said, as he poked his head through the door. "May I come in? I've brought you a night cap."

"I guess so. Come on in."

She took a seat on the chaise lounge and offered Deimos the ottoman. As soon as he was near her, her heart raced, and she felt the need to run. She took a deep breath to calm herself.

"That's a nice fire," Deimos said as he handed her one of two mugs he was carrying.

"What is it?" Ellie asked of the drink.

"Hot chocolate with a shot of liqueur. Try it. It's delicious."

Ellie took a sip. "Mmm. It is. Thank you."

"My pleasure." He took a drink, too.

"Where's Phobos?"

"Oh, he's around here somewhere, I'm sure."

Ellie took another sip of the chocolate.

"The truth is," Deimos said, "we drew lots to see who would get to visit you tonight, and, well, I won."

"You drew lots?" she repeated.

Deimos nodded.

"And Phobos agreed to this?"

"We both did."

"I see."

"I hope you aren't disappointed."

"Seems like the fairest way to decide things," she said.

"Not about that," Deimos said. "I hope you aren't disappointed that *I* won."

"Not at all."

She hadn't lied. The truth was, she was fascinated by them both.

"That's a relief," he said. "I thought maybe since you met him first that…Never mind. That's not what I want to talk about with you to-night."

"Then what do you want to talk about?"

"I know you know about the arrows."

Ellie felt her face get hot, and it wasn't from the fire or the warm chocolate.

Before she could reply, Deimos said, "And I want to reassure you that the last thing either of us wants is to hurt you or to see you hurt by someone else."

Not sure what to say, Ellie took another drink of the chocolate.

"I don't want you to feel any pressure whatsoever to respond to our—to my—feelings," he said. "But, with your permission, my brother and I would like to take turns spending time with you, so we can get to know you better, and so you can get to know us."

"I'd like that," she said.

Deimos grinned before he took a drink from his mug.

They sat in awkward silence for a moment as they drank from their mugs and gazed at the fire. Ellie felt brave, even though she was in the presence of Panic. It was almost as if the other twin were nearby, cancel-ing the effects of the other.

"Well, you know that I like to play softball," she said. "What's something you like to do?"

"Hmm, let's see. Well, I collect art."

She hadn't seen that coming. "What kind of art?"

"Paintings—mostly abstract. I tried creating my own once, but it was terrible." He laughed.

Ellie laughed, too. "I bet it wasn't that bad."

"Oh, it was."

They each took another drink from their mugs.

"What do you like about art? What attracts you to it?" Ellie asked.

"I guess it's the way we can find meaning in colors and shapes, even when there may be no meaning to be found. I can stare at some works for, well, not hours and hours—I don't have the luxury—but for quite a long while."

"If you don't create your own art, where do you find it?"

"I've been to all of the big metropolitan galleries all over the world. I used to go at least once a year. But, lately, I've enjoyed finding the lesser-known, more obscure artists. I'm always on the lookout for great art, and when I find something that stumps me, I buy it."

Ellie supposed gods had unlimited economic resources. Must be nice.

"What about music?" Ellie asked. "Do you like music?"

"Oh, yeah. In fact, a friend of mine recently introduced me to the music of a new popstar. Maybe you've heard of her? She has a unique sound. Goes by Juicy Jenkins."

Ellie beamed. "That's my favorite artist!"

"Oh, really? I'm especially fond of 'Take it Off.' Have you heard that one?"

"It's my very favorite on her newest album!"

"So, we have something in common," Deimos said with a grin. "What a relief."

They each took a drink from their mugs.

"I should take you to a gallery sometime," Deimos said.

"Or you could show me your personal collection," Ellie suggested. "I'd love to see the pieces that stumped you."

Deimos gave her his charming smile. "I'd like that very much."

Ellie felt awkward but brave. She wasn't sure how long she had before one of the Olympian gods would come to kill her, so she wanted to enjoy as much of what little time she had as possible.

"You can come closer, if you'd like," she said, patting the lounge.

He didn't need to be invited twice. As he sat beside her, so close that their legs touched, his musky scent and the reflection of the fire in his blue eyes excited her. She fought the urge to run, and fought the urge to slap him, by focusing on the loveliness of his deep blue eyes.

Maybe it was the liqueur, or perhaps it was her fear of death— whatever it was, Ellie set down her nearly empty mug and whispered, "I can't get over how beautiful you are."

Then Deimos closed his eyes and sighed, as though he were taking in the sensation of being so close to her. She watched his lips part, and she reeled in the pleasure of knowing that this gorgeous god was affected by her. By the time he opened his deep blue eyes again, she was aroused.

He glanced down at her breasts. Her nipples had become so taut that they were visible through the delicate fabric of her nightgown.

His hand moved toward her breast, but before he touched her, he hesitated, changed his mind.

She wished he wouldn't fight it. In her mind, she begged, *Kiss me.*

Then he set down his mug, and his broad arms circled her waist and pulled her hard against him as his mouth gently caressed hers.

As their lips touched, a chorus of moans escaped from their throats. Ellie moved her fingers through his thick hair and accepted his tongue into her mouth.

Overcome with sensual desire, Ellie was shocked when Deimos stopped.

"Thank you," he said gently. "I will cherish the taste of you all night."

"You don't have to leave," she said, trying not to sound too eager.

He pressed his lips to hers once more. "You need your rest. It's been a long day. And you've had a lot to take in."

She wasn't ready for him to go, but she refused to beg as she watched him leave.

"Keep the door open a crack, for the kitties," she said.

"Goodnight, Ellie."

"Goodnight, Deimos."

She climbed into the big canopy bed, still thinking of Deimos's mouth, his hands, his eyes, his broad shoulders. She hadn't been lying beneath the covers long when one of the tabbies joined her on the bed.

"There you are!"

She pulled him close for a kiss, and, as she stroked his fur, noticed the white patch on his left hindfoot. "Where's your friend?"

The kitty licked her cheek before curling up beside her.

"Thank goodness you came back," she said. "I missed you so much."

She reached up and turned off the bedside lamp and said, "Goodnight, kitty. Sweet dreams. I wish sweet dreams for the both of us."

Ellie yawned and closed her eyes, but she could still see Deimos smiling down at her with his beautiful eyes and parted lips. She lay there for many hours wishing he had stayed.

When Ellie awoke the next morning, she was pleased to see the orange tabby still curled up beside her, though she wondered where the other one had gone off to.

"Good morning," she said when the cat opened his eyes.

The tabby licked her cheek.

Ellie lay there for a minute, playing over in her mind all that had happened to her since the night she'd gone out to meet Gabe and Andrew. She hadn't ruled out the possibility that she was having a drug-induced trip or a psychotic breakdown, or that she was somehow trapped in a bizarre dream.

"This seems so real," she muttered as she stroked the cat.

The tabby licked her hand.

"I should be terrified," she said. "But I'm not. All I can think about is Deimos."

The cat nuzzled against her neck and purred.

"I know what I need," she said suddenly, throwing off her bed covers. "A run. I wonder if there are any sneakers with those fancy shoes."

Then she remembered that she only had to wish for something for it to appear. Sure enough, a pair of sneakers neatly lay on the floor beside her bed.

"And some athletic wear?" she asked aloud.

She glanced around the room and saw a pair of black yoga pants and a purple hoodie draped across the chaise lounge. The black pants had a colorful stripe of purple, pink, and white along the outer seams.

"My favorite colors," she said cheerfully.

Finding socks and underwear in one of the dresser drawers, Ellie changed from her nightgown. She noticed the kitty's eyes on her the whole time.

"Silly kitty," she said. "You sure are curious, aren't you, boy?"

Once she was dressed, she went to the bathroom and pulled her hair into two tight buns. Her sister used to tell her she looked like Mini Mouse when Ellie wore her hair this way, but Ellie's teammates loved it. Some of them had even copied her.

"Are you coming, too, kitty?" Ellie asked as she neared the door.

The tabby jumped from the bed and darted down the hall, disappearing around the corner.

"Wait for me!" Ellie called out, but when she reached the grand foyer, the cat was nowhere to be found.

Ellie wandered through a few of the rooms, saying, "Here, kitty, kitty."

When she reached the library, she noticed the gold chest wrapped in chains and wondered if the helm of invisibility was in it. Psyche had said it was the one thing that could protect Ellie from the other gods.

Suddenly, Ellie wondered if going for a run was a good idea.

"Good morning," Deimos said as he entered the library. Like her, he was wearing athletic clothes and sneakers. "Did you sleep well last night?"

Despite the sudden surge of adrenaline through her body, her increased heartrate, and her desire to run or punch him, Ellie recalled the feel of his lips on hers, of her breasts pressed against his chest, and blushed. "Yes. You?"

"Best sleep I've had in years."

In her head, Ellie said, *It might have been even better if you'd stayed*, but aloud, she said, "Me, too."

"You look adorable with your hair like that," he said. "I love it."

"Thanks."

"I was just about to head out for my morning run," he said. "Care to join me?"

"Seriously?" It would have been impossible for Ellie to smile any bigger. "I'd love to, if you think it's safe."

"Cupid put extra protections around the perimeter. Follow me. I know all the best trails."

He led her through the dining room and into the kitchen, where the satyr appeared to be cooking breakfast.

"Good morning, Deacon," Deimos said.

"Good morning," the satyr said, less enthusiastically than the god of panic.

"Smells delicious," Deimos added.

"It isn't for you. It's for her."

"Me?" Ellie asked. She didn't usually eat breakfast.

"It will be ready in twenty minutes," the satyr said. "I was going to take it up to your room, unless you'd like to eat it in the dining room."

"She'll take it in the dining room today, won't you, Ellie?" Deimos asked.

Ellie nodded.

"Thank you, Deacon," Deimos said as he continued through the kitchen toward the back door.

Ellie followed Deimos into the back garden, which was as elaborate as the front with its trellises of climbing roses bordered by flowering shrubs and fruit trees. They passed beneath an arbor covered in wisteria vine and followed a path down the hillside, where they both began to jog.

Once Ellie was running behind Deimos, she found it difficult to take in the glorious view from the mountain of the countryside below and of the sea beyond, because Deimos had the most perfectly shaped bottom she'd ever seen. And his biceps looked so good bulging beneath the shirt that clung to his body.

It was chilly this high on the mountain, but the purple hoody kept Ellie warm as she followed Deimos along the winding path around trees and large boulders. They ran all the way to the stream, where they stopped to catch their breath—though Deimos seemed fine. Only Ellie was panting.

"You okay?" he asked her.

She nodded. "Ask me after we make it back up."

"You take the lead this time," Deimos said. "Whenever you're ready."

Although she was disappointed to lose her spectacular view of his spectacular bottom, she led him up the winding path back toward the castle, trying to maintain a faster pace to impress him. In the back of her mind, though, she doubted there was much a mortal could do to impress a god. He only loved her because Cupid had shot him in the heart.

After their run, Deimos had coffee with Ellie in the dining room while she ate the eggs and bacon the satyr had cooked for her. Ellie offered some of her breakfast to Deimos, but he wasn't hungry. When she'd eaten as much as she could, Deimos asked her if she'd like to see some of his art.

"Is it safe to leave the castle?" Ellie asked.

"We don't need to," he said. "I'm a god, remember? I brought a few of my favorite pieces over from my London flat this morning. They're hanging upstairs in my room."

Ellie thanked Deacon as he cleared away her dishes, and then, together, she and Deimos headed upstairs to his suite.

As soon as they'd entered, he pulled off his sneakers and tossed each one into a corner of the room. Then he pulled off his socks and tossed them in the corner, too. Ellie began to wonder how far down he planned to strip when she noticed a white patch of skin on his left foot.

"What happened there?" she asked.

"Oh, that? I got that a long time ago when Phobos and I broke into the lair of a witch named Circe. She's a bit of an outcast. Lives on her own on an island, where she practices dark magic."

"Dark magic?"

"They say she waits for marooned sailors, seduces them, and then turns them into pigs, which she later eats."

"Gross!"

"Our parents warned us to avoid her island, so, of course, Phobos and I had to check it out." Deimos laughed.

"So how did you get that scar?"

"Right." Deimos laughed again. "This is where Phobos usually says, 'Get to the point, Professor Deimos.'"

Ellie laughed with him. She could imagine Phobos saying that very thing.

"See, we'd made it through her freaky forest, past her six wolves and six mountain lions, all the way through an open window at the back of the house when…"

"Can't gods just appear where they want to?" Ellie asked, wondering why he and his brother had had to sneak in through a window.

"God-travel comes with risks," Deimos explained. "That's why most of the gods have chariots."

"Oh. Sorry, I didn't mean to interrupt."

"Don't apologize. I love answering questions. They don't call me Professor Deimos for nothing."

They shared another laugh. Ellie was charmed by his smile and the twinkle in his deep blue eyes. Then she became distracted by his mouth.

"So, back to the scar." Deimos cleared his throat. "I'd climbed in through the window first, and before I'd got my head in, I felt something grab my foot."

"Was it Circe?"

"It was. And she had poison on her hand—some kind of dark magic. It burned like hell, right through my boot, nearly paralyzing me. Phobos saw what was happening and pulled me free, and we flew out of there as fast as we could. I've had this scar ever since."

"Your brother saved you," Ellie said. "How sweet."

"It's usually the other way around. I've saved him plenty."

"You two tease each other a lot, but you love each other, don't you?"

"He's my brother," Deimos said. "My best friend."

Ellie wished she and her sister felt the same. She'd always felt estranged from Dominique. They'd lived under the same roof, but they'd rarely spoken to one another, and when they had, they'd fought.

"That's what makes this situation so hard," Deimos added. "I know that every time I touch you," Deimos cupped her cheek, "and every time I kiss you," Deimos pressed his soft lips against her cheek, "it hurts him."

Ellie sighed. Then she whispered, "That feels so good."

Deimos kissed her lips, this time lingering. Ellie didn't want it to end.

"I won't tell if you won't." She moved her hands to his hard shoulders and kissed him back.

Deimos pulled away and said, "Would you like to see my art?"

"Um, sure," she said, trying to hide her disappointment.

Ellie didn't know much about art, but she enjoyed listening to Deimos explain what he liked about the works in his collection.

"I like this one," Ellie said of a painting of a runner in silhouette.

"What is that draws you in?" Deimos asked.

"I like that you can't tell whether she's running toward you or away from you. It's like you get to choose."

"That's what I love most about art," Deimos said with a smile. "I'm not talented enough to paint my own, so I like when I get to have a say in what it means."

Ellie loved how deeply Deimos thought. "You're a pretty interesting dude."

Deimos laughed. "That's the best compliment I've had in ages."

Ellie sucked in her lips, suddenly feeling shy and not sure what to say.

"I want you to have the painting," Deimos said of the runner. "I'll move it to your room, and you can take it with you when you go."

"Seriously?" Ellie hadn't expected he would give her such a beautiful and meaningful gift. "That's so nice. Thank you."

"I hope you'll think of me each time you look at it."

"I'm sure I will."

After showing her the rest of his art collection and explaining why he liked each painting, Deimos and Ellie returned to the back garden and sat on a bench beneath a tree, where they talked all afternoon. Deimos told her more stories about the gods and goddesses of Mount Olympus, and she told him stories from her childhood. He asked her questions about her favorite foods, colors, fashions, people, animals, and climate. Some answers she knew right away; others required more thought.

From where they sat, they had gorgeous views of the Greek countryside and the sea beyond. However, if asked to choose, Ellie would say the man beside her was the best view of all.

Around three-thirty, after they'd discussed capitalism, socialism, politics, religion, civil rights, and the shortcomings of different systems of education—topics she'd given very little thought to before today—Deimos asked her if she would like tea. He explained that he and his brother often took a light tea in the afternoon, a habit they formed not long after they'd purchased their London flat.

She joined him in a sitting room near the front of the castle, on the opposite side of the foyer from the library. She'd walked through the room that morning when she'd been looking for the orange tabby before their run, but she hadn't spent any significant time in it until now. The large arched window looked out to the front garden and provided a view of the fountain and statuary. Rich fabric of orange and golds hung on either side of the window, matching the patterned fabric on the sofas and chairs.

Their tea was served on a coffee table. They sat side by side on one of the sofas and ate bread and butter with jam while they sipped their hot tea. Ellie soon learned there was no such thing as light conversation with Deimos. He enjoyed more serious topics, such as whether freedom was an illusion.

Although Ellie hadn't given much thought to most of the topics they discussed, she enjoyed being challenged to think about them. She was especially fascinated when Deimos helped her to see something in a whole new way.

For example, he said that humankind was interesting in that often people who are the most limited—by social class, race, poverty, disease, politics—often believe they're free, while people who have greater privileges and liberties often believe they are trapped and powerless.

"You think so deeply," she said. "I like that."

"I like that you like that," he said with a smile.

After tea, Deimos walked Ellie back to her room, so she could rest before dinner.

He followed her in and took her hands. "Thank you for spending the day with me."

She smiled up at him, his blue eyes quelling the panic his touch aroused in her. "It was my pleasure. Thank you for making it so nice."

He studied her face and hair for a few quiet seconds before he sighed and then gently kissed her.

"What's wrong?" she asked against his lips. He seemed sad.

"My turn with you is coming to an end. Tonight, you dine with Phobos."

"Won't you be there too? And Cupid and Psyche?"

"Gods don't need as much food as mortals. We don't eat every day. It's the same with sleep. Cupid and Psyche are away from the castle, performing their duties."

"Oh. But if Phobos's turn begins at dinnertime, why not stay with me until then?" she asked with a flirtatious smile.

He squeezed her hands. "You need your rest."

She pulled him further into her room. "Come and lay by me while I nap."

He allowed her to pull him toward the bed, but she could tell he had reservations.

"Unless you don't want to," she added.

"Dear gods, of course I do," he muttered. "I enjoy being tormented in the afternoon."

"Tormented?" Why would he say that?

He moved his hands to her shoulders.

His elbows hung close to her breasts, nearly touching them. She longed for him to take her in his arms and pull her hard against him.

Instead, he kissed her on the forehead and said, "Until tomorrow night."

CHAPTER TWELVE

Phobos

Ellie pulled off her hoodie and yoga pants and lay in her underwear beneath the covers in the canopy bed, wondering why Deimos was holding back. If Cupid's arrow had really worked, wouldn't Deimos give anything to sleep with her?

Suddenly it occurred to her that maybe Deimos didn't want to take their relationship to the next level until Phobos had had a chance to win Ellie's heart.

On the heels of that thought was another: Deimos's love for his brother was as strong as his love for her, though they were different kinds of love.

With all these confusing thoughts running through her head, Ellie doubted she would fall asleep. She was delighted, when, moments later, the orange tabby with the white foot hopped onto the bed to cuddle with her.

"Where have you been, you silly thing? And where is your friend? I haven't seen him since yesterday."

The kitty licked her hand and nestled against her. The feel of his warm little body against her and of his little heart beating alongside her own was a comfort.

Two hours later, Ellie, dressed in the emerald satin gown with the high neck and very low back, headed for the stairs to the grand foyer. Phobos stood at the bottom of the steps waiting for her, just as he had the night before. He was wearing his tux, but with a white bowtie instead of the black. His blue eyes shined brightly up at her, and his luscious lips parted into a smile.

"Are you a beaver?" Phobos asked as Ellie descended. "Because dam!"

"Very funny!"

"If I didn't know better, I'd say you were the primary reason for global warming."

Ellie laughed. "They don't call it that anymore. It's called climate change."

The closer she got to him, the more difficult it became to quell the fear and to remember to breathe. She willed herself to smile and to appear light-hearted.

As she reached the ground floor, he took her hand and twirled her around. "If you were a library book, I'd check you out."

"Did you just Google a bunch of pickup lines?"

"Are you kidding? I'm a god. I don't need Google." Then he added, "Except when I'm lost. Then I use Google Maps."

Ellie laughed again as he led her to the dining room, where places for two had been set, along with a bottle of wine and a lit candle atop a slender bronze candlestick. Phobos pulled out a chair for her at the head of the table, where Cupid had sat the night before. Once she was seated, he took Psyche's chair and reached for the bottle of wine.

"Care for some of Dionysus's best?" he asked her.

"Dionysus is the wine god, right?" Ellie asked. "Deimos told me about him."

"I bet he did, along with fifty-five other things you didn't want to know."

"At one point he stopped himself and said, 'This is where Phobos would say, *Get to the point, Professor Deimos.*'"

Phobos chuckled as he filled their glasses, his blue eyes even bluer than she had remembered.

"My brother," he said. "You gotta love him. He's such a good-looking dude. Wouldn't you agree?"

"You're hilarious."

"Didn't I tell you?"

"And so different from your brother."

"Thank the gods for that. Just one of him is barely tolerable."

"You don't mean that."

Phobos cocked his head to the side. "Okay, see, now you're defending him. That's not a good sign—for me anyway."

"I'm not defending him," Ellie said, realizing his feelings were hurt. Maybe humor was a coping mechanism for him, like softball was for her. "I'm calling you out. I can tell you love him."

"What's not to love, with a face like that?" He gave her a cheesy smile.

Just then, Deacon entered with a plate of salad, which he placed before Ellie.

"Thank you," she said.

He gave her a nod and returned to the kitchen.

"Are you not having any?" she asked Phobos.

"Not tonight. I'm just here for the company."

She took a bite of the greens. "This salad is delicious." In her mind, she added, *And so are you.*

He smiled brightly and said, "I'm glad you think so."

"I'm getting better at controlling myself when I'm around you." She took a sip of wine.

Then, realizing how that sounded, she busted out laughing. Phobos did, too.

"I meant…"

He squeezed her arm. "I know what you meant. I'm sorry you have to work so hard when you're around me. I wish there was a way I could make you feel more comfortable."

"So, you do have a serious side," she teased before eating more of the salad.

"I wouldn't call it a *side*," he said with a grin. "More like a toe, or the nail on a toe."

She chuckled. "You don't share your brother's interest in discussing deep and serious subjects, like politics and poverty?"

"Not at all." Phobos drained his glass before pouring another. "I see no point in ruminating about things like poverty when there's nothing we can do about them. If I could, I'd dole out all the wealth in the world equally to everyone, but it's not in my power to do so."

"If gods can't do anything about it, who can?" she asked.

"People."

She raised her brows in surprise. "People?"

"Sure, the gods can inspire and maybe even guide mortals along, but, ultimately, it's up to them to make change—unless they're short on nickels and dimes."

Ellie grinned and shook her head. "You're on a roll tonight, aren't you?"

He stuck his hand under his chair and pulled up a dinner roll. "Oh, you're right."

Ellie slapped the table and guffawed.

"Let's pour you a little more wine." Phobos tilted the bottle to her glass. Then he said, "I may not be like my brother, but I do have deep thoughts every once in a while."

"Is that so?" Ellie took the last bite of the salad.

"Absolutely. For example, I've often thought the worst possible time for a mortal to have a heart attack would be while playing charades."

Ellie covered her mouth and shook her head again.

"Think about it. Can you imagine?" He grinned.

"You're killing me," she said. "My face actually hurts from smiling so much."

"Good. I'm working very hard to undo my natural effect on you."

She realized then that everything he'd said so far had been for her, to help her to laugh rather than to quake in fear.

"That salad was delicious." She moved the plate aside.

"Does that mean you're ready for the next course?"

"I'm stuffed. I can't eat another bite."

"Already? Are you sure you aren't a goddess? You look like one and eat like one."

Ellie blushed. "I wish."

"Would you like to go for a walk? It's cold outside, but I'll keep you warm."

"Promise?"

He helped her from her chair. "I swear on the River Styx."

"What does that mean?"

"You can ask Professor Deimos tomorrow night. Let's go."

Phobos placed his hand on the small of her back—dangerously close to the top of her exposed crack—which caused her nipples to go taut. She glanced down, and, sure enough, they were pointing toward the front door.

Once she and Phobos were out in the cold night, Phobos came up behind her and wrapped his arms around her waist. "Let me know if it gets too hot for you."

His warm breath on the back of her neck made her shiver.

"You okay?" he asked.

Heat radiated from him like an electric blanket.

"Mmm," she said. "That feels nice."

She gazed up at the thousands of brilliant stars above them. They seemed close enough to touch.

"Walking might be difficult in this position," Phobos said. "So, if you don't mind…"

Holding her tight, he lifted off the ground, taking her with him, as he hovered a few feet in the air.

Ellie's stomach dropped. "Whoa!"

"I've got you," he whispered into her ear, his hot breath sending shivers down her spine.

"Don't let me go," she said, feeling wobbly.

"Never."

She blinked her eyes, expecting to wake from a dream. "This is incredible."

"This is how a god takes a stroll around the garden," he said softly.

Slowly, he carried her just a few feet off the ground along the hillside, weaving around the trees and shrubs with ease.

"One of my shoes just fell off," Ellie said with a laugh.

"Where? Oh, I see it."

The shoe magically returned to her foot, startling her.

"Thanks!" she said.

Then he flew her around the back of the castle, past the bark bench where she and Deimos had spent the afternoon, and back to the front door of the castle, where he gently set her down on her feet.

She turned in his arms to face him, resting her hands on his chest. "Thank you. That was amazing."

"Check out Selene," he said, pointing at the moon. "You can't tell it from here, but she's riding her silver chariot across the sky."

"That's not what my astronomy professor said," she teased.

"Professors don't know everything."

She laughed. "Including Professor Deimos?"

Phobos sighed—not with pleasure, but with annoyance.

"I'm sorry," Ellie said. "It's your turn tonight, and I keep mentioning your brother. I only meant to make a joke."

"I keep mentioning him, too. It's not your fault."

"Then what's bothering you?"

He stroked her hair. "I just wish it weren't so obvious that you're already in love with him."

Ellie's mouth fell open. "What?"

"It's okay. I'm glad it happened to *one* of us. No use *both* of us being miserable."

"Phobos…"

"Let's get you inside."

"Wait. Listen to me for a minute."

He gazed down at her, trying to hide his disappointment, but failing miserably.

"Remember when I asked Cupid if he'd struck me with an arrow?"

Phobos nodded.

"I asked him that because ever since you saved me from your mother by the stream, ever since you held me on your lap beneath the rocks, I've wanted to kiss you."

Phobos searched her eyes, as if he wasn't sure he believed her.

"Please, Phobos. I…"

Unlike Deimos, who'd gently pressed his lips to hers as if she were a fragile thing, Phobos pushed her against the front door, pinned her arms above her head, and ravished her mouth with his.

Ellie gasped as she felt a pulse deep inside, between her legs, where she was suddenly hot and wet.

He took her bottom lip between his teeth, then left her mouth to kiss her neck. His tongue swept across her ear, and she moaned with delight.

"Let's get you inside, out of the cold," he said as he kissed her hair.

"Don't stop," she begged.

He pressed his hands against her bare back and pulled her hard against him. As he kissed her other ear, his hands moved down her back and brushed across the top of her bottom.

"Mmm," she moaned, as her knees buckled beneath her.

He caught her and carried her inside, to a couch in the library, where he laid her on her back before kneeling on the floor beside her. She gazed up at him with hooded eyes, feeling as though she were only half awake and holding onto a dream.

He bent over her and kissed her, using his lips to tug at her lips, and sometimes using his teeth. He was turning her on, making her crazy for him.

She ran her fingers through his vibrant red hair. He stroked her face and then moved his hands down the emerald satin gown to stroke her breasts.

"Dear, God," she whispered.

Suddenly, he stopped kissing her and jumped to his feet.

She sat up. "What's wrong?"

He raked his fingers through his hair. "I lost control."

She smiled up at him. "So?"

"I made a promise."

"Huh?"

He sat on the couch near her feet, and then he slid himself closer, holding her legs on his lap. "Deimos and I promised each other we'd give you time to get to know us before either of us got physical with you."

While Ellie admired the twins' respect for one another, she'd was aching for him to touch her again. "Oh."

"I'm sorry," Phobos said as he cradled her legs. "He's always been the twin with better self-restraint."

She put a hand on his broad shoulder and gave him a smile. "I'm glad you lost control, Phobos."

He chuckled. "I'm glad you're glad." Then, he added, "Since *Cupid* can't choose between us, we're hoping *you* might."

"What do you mean Cupid can't choose between you?"

"He could drive an arrow through your heart and make you fall in love with one of us, but he can't choose which of us he should make more miserable than the other."

"More miserable? Don't you mean happier?"

Phobos shrugged. "For a little while. Until you die."

Ellie didn't know what to say.

Then he asked, "Can I get you something? More wine? Some dessert?"

She glanced across the room at the gold chest wrapped in chains. "Can I see the helm again?"

"Isn't there anything else I can get you?" he asked. "Like a really good book from this amazing collection?"

"How do you know it's amazing? Have you even *read* any of these books?"

"I've read *all* of the novels, including many more in my own library in London. The nonfiction is more Deimos's thing. He wants to know everything about the world, and I want to escape it."

"I see." Ellie studied his thoughtful profile, wondering what he wasn't saying. "Which book is your favorite?"

"My *favorite*? You may as well ask me which of your eyes I find more beautiful."

Ellie grinned. "Are you saying you can't choose?" She understood the feeling. As magical as Phobos had made her feel tonight, she hadn't stopped thinking of Deimos.

"I used to think I was indecisive, but now, I'm not so sure," he said with a smile.

"Are you trying to be funny again?"

"Only if it's working."

"Why can't I see the helm?"

"There's something else I want you to see." He stood up and offered her his hand.

She took it and climbed to her feet. "Where are we going?"

"Do you like to swim?"

"I guess, but I'm not that good at it."

"It's my favorite thing to do," he said. "Or was, pre-arrow. I used to enjoy chasing the sea nymphs around the seven seas. If I could catch one, she'd let me kiss her."

"Oh, really. You're *that* kind of guy?"

"*Was* that kind of guy. Come on."

He led her from the library through the grand foyer, and just before the wide cased opening leading to the dining room, he stopped and motioned toward a door in the side of one of the staircases.

"Open it," he said.

"Okay, but I'm scared."

"I have that effect on people."

She turned the knob and pulled open the door, revealing another set of stairs. "A basement?"

"Basement, dungeon, same difference." He waved his hand and said, "After you."

As she descended the first few steps, she told herself that this is exactly where a serial killer would lead his prey. Why was she making it so easy for someone to kill her? What did she really know about Phobos, anyway?

She supposed if her captors wanted her dead, they would have killed her by now.

Halfway down the stairs, she understood what Phobos wanted to show her: down below was an Olympic-size swimming pool.

"Who has a swimming pool in their basement?" she said in disbelief.

"Your expectations of the gods aren't very high."

"I didn't even know you existed until Cupid and Psyche brought me here."

"I shouldn't be surprised. It's the fault of the gods, not you."

Before Ellie could ask him what he meant, Phobos took her hand and led her to the edge of the pool. Although the room was dark and cavernous, the pool shimmered, as if bathed in moonlight.

"In the mood for a swim?" he asked with a twinkle in his eyes.

"I'm not an expert launderer, but I have a feeling this gown would be ruined if I swam in it."

"No one's suggesting you should."

"Are you asking me to skinny dip with you?"

"If 'skinny dip' means 'swim without clothes,' then yes."

Ellie's mouth dropped open. As much as she wanted to see this beautiful god in all his glory, she was afraid. Maybe it was the effect he was having on her as the god of fear. "Aren't you worried you'll lose control with me again?"

"I'm constantly worried I'll lose control with you." Then he grinned. "Oh, I get it now. You aren't aware that I can see through your clothes."

Her right hand flew to her breasts and her left to her crotch. "What? You can?"

"Ellie, what am I?"

"Uh, you're a god? The god of fear?"

"Yes. And gods can see through walls. We can see through rock. Unless something is marked with a ward of protection by another god, we can see through it. Don't you think we can see through a flimsy piece of fabric? And, in case you were wondering, I can see through your hands, too."

CHAPTER THIRTEEN

Promises

Ellie stepped out of the emerald satin gown, leaving it where it fell, walked to the pool's edge in nothing but her panties, and took the three stone steps into the shallow end.

"It's warm!" she cried gleefully. She went down on her knees, so that the water reached her neck. The warm water soothed her, countering the effect the god of fear had on her. "It feels good!"

Phobos stood over her, smiling down at her.

"Your turn!" she shouted.

She was shocked when Phobos, still in his tux, lifted off the ground and flew above the deep end of the pool, about ten feet in the air. He held his arms out, legs straight, and back arched, and began to drop in a swan dive. Just as his body hit the water, his shoes and clothing vanished. Ellie barely caught a glance at the god's muscular backside before he submerged. And she hadn't even blinked when his head reappeared above the water inches from her.

"Show off," she teased.

He laughed as he pushed his wet hair away from his face, his bicep gleaming in the faux moonlight. When he stood up, the water barely reached his waist. Although the pool distorted her view of the lower half of his body, his bare, broad chest excited her. She wanted to stand up, too, and go to him, but she was afraid.

"So, how many sea nymphs have you kissed?" she asked, playfully batting her eyes.

He laughed again as he knelt in the water beside her, without touching her. "Why do you want to know? Jealous?"

"What if I am?"

"What about you?" he asked, avoiding her question. "How many boys have you kissed?"

Exactly two, she thought. Deimos and Phobos. "Are we counting cousins and nephews?"

"Only if they were your lovers."

"Ooh. Gross." She splashed a little water in his face.

"Are you challenging me to a water fight?" he asked with a grin.

"Maybe. I haven't decided yet."

He cocked his head to the side, reminding her of the orange tabby she hadn't seen for two days.

"Promise to go easy on me?" she asked.

"Why would I do that?"

"Because you're a god, and I'm…"

"An exceptional athlete, who loves competition?"

He hit the water, and she turned just as it washed over the back of her head, soaking her hair.

"You asked for it," she said playfully, as she scooped the water toward him with both hands.

But, in an instant, he was behind her, pinning her arms behind her back. Still kneeling on the pool floor, she could see the tops of her breasts swelling at the surface.

"That's not fair," she breathed.

Phobos knelt behind her with his body close. Still pinning her arms, he kissed her neck.

Ellie closed her eyes and gasped.

Phobos released her arms to cup her breasts. "I'm sorry. I can't help myself."

Ellie leaned back against him. "Don't apologize."

His hands caressed her breasts and abdomen, lighting her on fire.

She was about to beg him not to stop when he vanished, leaving her alone in the pool.

Dumbfounded, she scanned the cavernous room and found him standing on the pool's edge wearing a white robe. He held a second one folded across one arm.

"I'm sorry," he said again as he held open the other robe for her.

Ellie climbed the three stone steps, feeling his gaze on her as she slipped into the robe. It was warm, like it was fresh out of a dryer. "Thank you."

He led her back to the library, where they sat on the couch in their robes together. With a wave of his hand, Phobos made a fire in the hearth.

"Are you warm enough?" He slid his arm along the back of the couch and around her shoulders.

"Mmm-hmm."

"Can I get you anything? Something hot to drink, maybe?"

"Ooh, some hot chocolate would be nice."

He grinned "With or without a little somethin'-somethin'?"

"With."

He disappeared and reappeared with a mug in each hand. "Here you go."

Still a little dazed, Ellie blinked several times before accepting the mug. "Thanks."

He returned his arm to her shoulders along the back of the couch and clinked his mug to hers. "Cheers."

She took a sip of the soothing chocolate and then said, "I want to know everything about you."

Cupid sat beside his father in the throne room belonging to Hades, the lord of the Underworld. Hades sat on his throne picking at his black curly beard as he considered what Ares had said.

"I'm not a fan of murder," Hades said, "especially when it's done by a god on an innocent."

Cupid was relieved to hear that. It was a good sign.

Hades continued, "Megaera, Alecto, and Tisiphone take their duties as the avengers of murder very seriously."

"As they should," Ares said.

Hades crossed one leg over the other and sat further back in his chair. "Tiresias warned us that our interference would only hasten this…what did he call it?"

"The reckoning," Cupid said.

"The old seer did, indeed," Ares said.

Hades clapped his hands together once. "Then I propose we do nothing."

Cupid exchanged a worried glance with his father.

"You disagree?" Hades asked.

"It's a little too late for that," Ares explained. "Aphrodite acted before we had all the information."

"What did she do?"

Cupid listened solemnly as his father explained what had happened with Ellie Beaufort.

When Ares had finished, Hades uncrossed his legs and sat up in his chair. "Then the prophecy is already well on its way to becoming fulfilled."

"I'm afraid so," Ares said.

"If only we knew more about it," Hades said. "You should consult with Apollo. And I'll send a message to Persephone, to ask her to speak with Hecate."

"That's precisely what we've come to ask you not to do, Lord Hades," Cupid said.

Hades furrowed his dark brows. "Whatever for?"

When Ares didn't reply, Cupid said, "Because we fear the other Olympians will try to kill Ellie, hoping to thwart the fulfillment of the prophecy."

"Leaving my twin sons heartbroken years earlier than is necessary," Ares added.

"But they will be heartbroken, nevertheless," Hades said. "Why keep this information from the others when the girl will live, at the most, for another seventy years—a mere blink of an eye to you and me?"

"My father asked me the same question," Cupid said. "But I feel guilty for burdening my brothers with this eternal misery. I want time to search for a way to free them."

"I thought it was impossible," Hades said.

"I can't accept that," Cupid said. "I've come here to ask you this favor: Please keep the information about the prophecy, about the reckoning, a secret. As you pointed out, we can't do anything to prevent its coming, but the others might not see it that way. They'll want to kill Ellie Beaufort."

"Some of them, perhaps," Hades said.

"As long as the mortal lives," Cupid continued, "I'll do everything in my power to find a cure for my brothers. If you'll agree, I'll owe you, Lord Hades. I promise to come through for you, if you should ever need me."

"What of Apollo?" Hades asked. "Have you secured a promise from him?"

"Not yet," Ares admitted. "He's gone to Delphi and hasn't returned, but we plan to see him as soon as he does."

"I give you my word," Hades said. "I'll share what I know with no one."

Cupid climbed to his feet and bowed deeply before the lord of darkness. "Thank you, Lord Hades. I'm very grateful."

Hades nodded his head once and then said, "Now, about my helm."

"Yes?" Ares asked.

"I want it back," Hades said.

Over the next few weeks, Deimos and Phobos alternated spending time with Ellie, but Phobos never again touched her like he had in the pool. The boys even refrained from kissing Ellie, except for an occasional peck on her cheek or forehead. They were trying to honor their promise to each other to avoid being physical with her until she'd had a chance to get to know them. Ellie found herself both exhilarated and frustrated in their company. At bedtime, she would tell whichever tabby had found his way back to her bed how crazy the twins were making her and how badly she wished they would kiss her again.

Ellie began each day with a run with one of the twins. Around eleven-thirty, they would enjoy a visit in the beautiful garden while she ate lunch. Deimos tended to enjoy serious topics, whereas Phobos liked to keep the conversation light and humorous. Later, around four-thirty, they would have tea in the sitting room. Dinners were usually formal in the dining room at seven. Occasionally, Cupid and Psyche would join her and one of the twins. After dinner, they usually took a stroll through the garden or drank spiked hot chocolate before a warm fire in the library.

One afternoon on a bench beneath a tree, Ellie had just finished her lunch, when Deimos asked how she had managed to fail Freshman Composition, which she had mentioned in a previous conversation with him.

"I'm not dumb," she said defensively. "I just couldn't do the papers."

"Why not?" he asked. "Did you never learn how to write?"

She rolled her eyes. "I can write just fine."

"Then why didn't you?"

"Whenever I sat down with my laptop, my mind, it would go blank. I'd just panic." Ellie's eyes widened as a new thought occurred to her. "Was that you, Deimos? Did you cause me to panic?"

She was surprised when his cheeks turned red.

"Probably," he said.

"What do you mean, 'probably'? Don't you know?"

"There are literally millions of you. I can't be expected to know and remember each and every one."

For the first time since she'd met him, she felt annoyed. "How can you live with yourself, knowing you're ruining people's lives."

"That's not on me, Ellie. Among other things, my job is to create challenges that build character. If everything in life was easy, nothing would matter."

Ellie thought about that for a minute, trying to decide if she agreed. Then she shook her head. "Please tell me you aren't trying to justify suffering. I grew up in the projects and sometimes went days without food. My mom seemed to never catch a break. I hate it when people say that suffering has purpose or that it builds character. The ones who say it ain't the ones suffering, I can tell you that. It's like they're trying to make themselves feel better for not doing anything about it."

Deimos took her hands. "I agree with you one hundred percent."

"You do?"

"But I need you to understand that my job isn't to cause suffering. I inspire people to run from danger or to fight it. Sometimes they run when they should fight."

"Are you saying that's what happened when I tried to write my papers? I ran?"

He squeezed her hands. "I think you run from a lot of things. Don't you?"

"I have depression. Why do people always want to blame victims of mental illness? My own mother says it's all in my head."

Deimos stroked his cheek. "You misunderstood me. I'm not talking about the depression—though I think you run from it, too, half the time, right? You don't see a doctor for it, do you?"

Ellie shook her head.

"I think you run from your unresolved issues," Deimos said. "And that just makes your depression worse."

Ellie pulled her hands from his, annoyed. "I don't have unresolved issues."

"Now you're just lying to yourself."

Ellie's mouth dropped open. *How dare you?* she thought.

"You love your mother, but you hate her too, and you hate that you hate her, because you know she doesn't deserve it."

Tears filled her eyes.

"But it's easier for you to ignore it—to run away from it all—than to go home and face your issues."

Ellie took a deep breath. He was right. Deimos had her pegged.

Although Ellie's conversations with Phobos were typically less intense, they did get around to the subject of suffering one afternoon while they were sunbathing by the stream.

Ellie said, "You once told me that the gods can't do anything about poverty—that it's up to people."

"Did I say that? How wise of me."

"Do you believe it?"

He threw a stone into the stream and made it skip five times.

"Good one," she said. "Let me try."

She found a flat rock and threw it with a backspin. "One, two, three, four, five, six! Beat you!"

He pulled her onto his lap and kissed the back of her hair. Then she turned and said, "So, answer me. Seriously. Do you really blame people for their poverty?"

"I don't blame the poor people, no. Most of them are trapped in a cycle that not even Hercules could break out of, if you ask me. They don't make enough money to pay the rent, and they can't keep a job because they keep getting evicted. It's a vicious cycle."

"Then how can you say people and not gods are to blame?"

"It's the greedy, wealthy, powerful people of the world. They don't want things to change. They want policies that ensure their wealth never gets redistributed."

"Not all wealthy people are greedy," she said.

"I'm not talking about the ones who work hard and reap the benefits," Phobos said. "I'm talking about the wealthy, powerful families who've held onto their power for generations."

Ellie wrinkled her nose. "Are you a communist?"

Phobos grinned. "Gods, no. But I'm not a fan of capitalism, either."

"Why can't the gods redistribute *their* wealth to the poor people of the world?"

"We tried that, more than once. The same thing always happens. A powerful king or dictator brainwashes subjects into following him, and he hoards the wealth. Every time we've tried that experiment, whole populations of people have been killed."

"Oh."

"Like I said, the gods can't solve the problem of poverty. It's up to people to figure it out."

Ellie studied Phobos's profile while he gazed out at the countryside below.

"You're pretty cute when you're serious," she said.

He grinned. "Is that so?"

She wanted him to kiss her so badly, but she just nodded.

"Then I'll have to try to be serious more often."

"Oh, Phobos. You're cute either way."

"Now you're just making me blush." He pecked her cheek before throwing another stone into the stream. "Aha! Six! Now we're even! I'm going for seven."

In the middle of her second week in the castle, Deimos surprised her one evening. They had spent a lot of time talking about family, and Ellie had admitted that she was afraid that her mother and sister might be worried about her. There was a chance they hadn't noticed Ellie was gone, since she was away at school; but if they had, they could be worried sick.

So that next evening, when Ellie went down to dinner, she found her mother, sister, and nephew waiting for her at the banquet table.

Deimos had told them the truth about everything. They were still in shock, but they were overjoyed to learn that Ellie was okay. Deimos gave up his time with Ellie to allow her to catch up with her family and to explain what had been happening to her. He returned a few hours later to take them home. Although Ellie was sad to say goodbye, she realized that, if given the choice, she would choose to remain with Phobos and Deimos. She was crushing on them so hard that she couldn't bear to be away from them. If she didn't have the cats to comfort her when she was alone at night, she would have snuck out of bed to persuade one of the twins to sleep with her.

But she didn't know which one she would choose.

Just before midnight, Deimos came to her room to tuck her in. He explained that Ellie's mother and sister wouldn't recall coming to the castle, but he'd left them with a letter written in Ellie's handwriting explaining that she'd needed a break from school and had left with a friend for a tour around the world. The letter promised she'd keep in touch. And Deimos had given them the feeling that Ellie was fine.

"I'll send her a postcard from time to time," Deimos said as he stroked Ellie's cheek.

She had a candle burning on the table beside her bed. "Will you blow out the candle for me?"

Deimos sat on the edge of her bed. "I don't think most people realize that you're not really trying to *blow* the flame. You're trying to smother it with carbon dioxide. The flame dies in the absence of oxygen."

"Your brains are so sexy, professor," she teased.

He leaned down and stroked her cheek again.

Ellie wished he'd give her a kiss goodnight, but, when he bent down to kiss her, it was to peck her on the forehead.

"Goodnight, Ellie," he said.

"Goodnight, Deimos. And thank you so much for bringing my family to me today. It meant everything to me."

He sighed and squeezed her hand. She could tell he was fighting the urge to kiss her or to say something he wanted to say. He pecked her on the cheek, extinguished the candle, and left.

A few days later, Phobos decided that he would surprise Ellie, too. He rounded up some of Ellie's favorite celebrity athletes and brought them to the castle to play a game of softball with her. He'd transformed the ballroom into a softball field. It looked and felt real. Even the grass and the dirt on the pitcher's mound seemed authentic.

Softball stars Lisa Fernandez, Caitlin Lowe, Jessica Mendoza, Dot Richardson, Cat Osterman, and Crystl Bustos, along with baseball stars Albert Pujols, Bryce Harper, David Ortiz, Alex Rodriguez, Clayton Kershaw, and Derek Jeter joined with some of Ellie's favorite athletes from other sports—Serena and Venus Williams, Shaquille O'Neal, and Peyton Manning.

Unlike Ellie's mother and sister, these athletes were led to believe they were having a dream. They broke up into two teams of mixed genders with nine players each, with Ellie and Phobos playing on opposite sides. It was thrilling for Ellie to pitch to her idols and role models. It was especially exciting to strike out Shaquille O'Neil. And it was hilarious when Phobos accidentally hit the ball too hard, busting it and the bat in the process. Luckily, he was a god and could conjure more balls and bats.

Ellie was sorry to see the exciting day come to an end. Phobos took the athletes home to their beds and returned to the castle in time to have dinner with Ellie.

Tonight, she wore a hot-pink, floor-length gown with a deep v-neck and no sleeves. Ellie enjoyed the chance to wear a different dress every night. The magical closet in her suite never ran out of clothes.

And she never tired of seeing the twins in their tuxedos. Phobos looked especially hot tonight, because he hadn't had time to shave, and it suited him well.

Ellie reached out and stroked his cheek. "I like this look."

"I'll have to remember that."

"You usually keep it shaved."

"The whiskers feel itchy, but I'll endure it for you."

"No. I want you to be comfortable in your own skin."

"You certainly look comfortable in yours," he said. "That color looks amazing on you."

"Check out my fingers and toes," she said. "I found polish to match."

"Sexy," he said with a grin.

"It's the color of cotton candy, I guess. Do you like cotton candy?"

"It's too sweet for me. And I don't like the texture." Then he leaned closer to her and whispered, "You, on the other hand, are the perfect combination of sweet and spicy, and I would love to eat you up."

Ellie kept her cool, but in her mind, she was begging him to put his money where his mouth was. She amended that thought with, *Hell, put me where your mouth is.*

She noticed the corners of his mouth twitch, and, for a moment, she feared she'd spoken out loud.

After she took a sip of her wine, she said, "Thank you for today, Phobos. That was the best gift anyone's ever given me."

Phobos's deep blue eyes sparkled in the candlelight. He gave her a wink and said, "It was my pleasure." Then he said, "I have something else for you."

He opened his hand, and a softball appeared.

"I had it signed by the athletes we played with today," he said as he handed it over to her.

Ellie's eyes widened with surprise. "Thank you so much, Phobos! What a thoughtful gift!"

His smile, his voice, his eyes—Ellie could barely contain herself. She wanted to reach across the table, take his vibrant red hair in her fists, and pull his mouth to hers. But she managed to keep her cool.

Later, alone with one of the tabbies, she confessed her heart's desires.

Ellie began to suspect that the twins bragged to each other about their surprises for her, because it soon appeared as if they were trying to outdo the other. One evening, a few days after the softball game, Deimos arranged for Juicy Jenkins and her band to come to the castle for a private concert. Juicy and her band played in the front sitting room, and Deimos and Ellie were the only spectators in attendance. She and Deimos had a blast dancing the night away. He was as good a dancer as he was a kisser.

At one point she said, "You got moves, Deimos. I like your moves."

"When you understand that dance is simply moving from one position to another to the rhythm of the music, it becomes quite easy."

"Thank you for that, Professor." She laughed.

After the private concert, after Juicy Jenkins and her band had been returned to their homes and had been convinced that they'd been dreaming, Deimos stood in the sitting room with Ellie in his arms, humming one of Juicy's slow tunes and swaying with Ellie back and forth. She looked up into his deep blue eyes longing for a kiss.

"I want to kiss you so badly," Deimos said. "But I need to keep my promise to Phobos."

Ellie buried her face in Deimos's neck and sighed.

Then two days later, Phobos surprised Ellie again by bringing her teammates to the castle for a swimming party. They were waiting for her in the basement after lunch, already playing a game of water volleyball. Popular tunes streamed in the background. A table of drinks and snacks, along with over a dozen outdoor loungers, had been placed along the perimeter of the pool.

When Ellie descended the basement steps, Phobos blew a whistle, and her teammates turned and shouted, "Surprise, Ellie!"

Ellie was flabbergasted. She turned to Phobos, "Thank you so much!"

Ellie and Phobos joined in the game of water volleyball, playing on opposite teams again. Although Phobos accidentally busted the ball a few times by forgetting his own strength, he eventually adjusted, just as he had during the softball game. Ellie enjoyed his competitive streak as they trash-talked to each other from opposite sides of the net.

It was hard to say goodbye to her friends when the party was over, but she was glad she wasn't leaving with them. She'd been happier at the castle with Phobos and Deimos than she had ever been in her life.

Once her teammates were gone, Phobos changed into a long white robe and offered Ellie one, too. They were just like the robes they had worn that night he had touched her breasts in the pool. He led her to the library, where he made a fire in the hearth. They sat snuggled together on the couch, sipping mugs of hot chocolate with a little "somethin'-somethin'" in them.

He stroked her hair. "Can I get you anything else?"

She wanted to say, "A kiss," but she needed to respect the promise the brothers had made to each other.

"You've already done so much," she said. "That was such a nice surprise. Thank you."

"I enjoy seeing you happy," he said before taking a sip from his mug.

When he said things like that, it made her question the reality of the moment, wondering again if this was all a drug-induced trip or a psychotic breakdown.

"How can you be so perfect?" she wondered out loud.

"I wouldn't say I'm perfect," he said with a grin. "Though, I *am* pretty close."

"Pretty damn close." She laughed.

"I could say the same of you."

He stroked her cheek. His lips were so close to hers that she could almost taste them.

She closed her eyes and thought, *Please, kiss me. You're driving me crazy.*

Ellie was shocked when he cradled her head and pulled her mouth to his. All the tension that had been building up between them seemed to explode in one luscious, feverish moment. He tugged at her lips with his, sending shocks of pleasure down her body. When he took her bottom lip between his teeth, she moaned.

He pulled away and clenched his jaw. "I'm sorry. I shouldn't have done that. I lost it again."

Bewildered, Ellie sank back in the couch. "Don't apologize. I wanted you to kiss me."

"I don't know how much longer I can keep my promise to my brother," he muttered. "It might be time to make you choose."

Ellie shook her head. "I…"

"You still can't choose? Gods, Ellie! It's been weeks."

"I know, I…"

"I'm sorry," he said. "I don't want to push you--at least, not until I'm sure that I'm the one you'll choose."

She squeezed his hand. "I know this isn't fair—to either one of you."

When she was with Phobos, she was convinced that he was the one for her; but, when she was with Deimos, she was certain *he* was the one. She loved how Phobos shared her competitive nature and how he made her laugh. But she also loved how Deimos challenged her to think more deeply about things. And she loved Deimos's sensitivity and his gentle touch.

She felt chemistry with them both. And she admired them equally.

"Let's talk about something else," Phobos said.

"Good idea." Ellie glanced across the room at the gold chest wrapped in chains. "Can I see the helm?"

Phobos sighed. "I can't show it to you *now*."

"Why not?"

"Because I can't, Ellie."

"But…"

"It's in use."

"What?" She could no longer quell the fear caused by his presence. She could barely breathe as she said, "I thought we needed it here, in case one of the other gods tries to kill me."

"I didn't say it wasn't *here*," he said cryptically.

Ellie took a deep breath, trying to hold herself together. If the helm was in use nearby, did that mean the person beneath the helm was in the room with them?

"Phobos? Are we being watched?"

Phobos sighed heavily. "Safety first, don't you agree?"

Ellie jumped to her feet, scanning the room for signs of another's presence. "Who's there?"

Phobos stood up and placed his hands on her shoulders. "Please understand…"

She pulled away from him and said, "Cupid? Psyche?"

She hoped to the gods it was Cupid or Psyche, because the thought of Deimos watching on as she and Phobos…

Ellie turned to Phobos. "Please tell me Deimos hasn't been with us all evening."

Deimos appeared across the room with the helm in his hands. "Ellie, I'm sorry. I…"

She didn't wait to hear what he had to say. Humiliated and horrified, she ran from the room.

CHAPTER FOURTEEN

A Warning

Cupid sat beside his father in his father's chariot as they headed toward Mount Olympus. Apollo had finally returned after having been gone for weeks on a mission at Delphi.

The clouds parted, and the gates opened. Ares drove the chariot into the garage. Cupid unbridled the horses and took them to their stalls. Then he met his father in the great hall.

Zeus sat on his throne at the back of the room chatting with his sister Hestia. Hera wasn't with him, probably because she and Psyche were performing their duties. Athena, who was rarely at home, was sharpening her sword while she spoke with Hephaestus. The other Olympians were either in their private rooms or away from Mount Olympus.

"Apollo's agreed to speak with us," Ares said when Cupid approached. "He's waiting for us in his chambers."

Cupid had never felt at ease with Apollo. The god could be hot and cold. Usually he was one of the more compassionate and helpful of the Olympians. As the god of truth, he could never lie, nor could another tell a falsehood in his presence without Apollo knowing. He was also the healer, if deities were ever damaged beyond their restorative powers. The consensus among the other gods was that Apollo had the loveliest voice and musical talents. They were also in agreement that Apollo was the most beautiful of the male deities, with forest-green eyes and wavy brown hair and the most perfect proportions of forehead to nose to cheeks to lips.

Apollo often used his beauty to seduce both male and female mortals and nymphs. This is where Cupid found the god to be hot and cold. Apollo could be loyal to one partner for decades; however, he could also be a cruel and selfish lover. He went through phases, and he'd often solicited Cupid's help, demanding that he make some poor nymph love Apollo. When Cupid refused, because it was his duty to refuse, Apollo would make Cupid sorry.

Cupid followed Ares into Apollo's main living room, where the god of truth and healing was lying on a couch eating a bunch of grapes while a golden harp was being played softly by a muse in the corner of the room.

"Come in," Apollo said without getting up. "Make yourselves comfortable."

They walked past a fountain to sit on the couch opposite Apollo. The god's bow and arrows lay strewn across the coffee table between them.

"Care for some grapes?" he asked them once they were seated.

"None for me, thanks," Ares said.

Cupid shook his head.

"Now tell me why you're here," Apollo said before popping another grape into his mouth.

Ellie ran into her room and closed the door behind her, still reeling with humiliation. She couldn't imagine why Phobos would knowingly be intimate with her in front of Deimos, or why Deimos would let him.

Pulling the white robe closer around her, Ellie wished for a fire in the hearth and then curled up in front of it on the green chaise lounge. She was surprised when one of the tabbies hopped off the canopy bed and joined her.

She couldn't be happier to have a friend as she whisked him up in her arms and gave him a hug and kiss. "I've missed you, kitty. Have you been in here all evening?"

When she looked at him more closely, she noticed he was missing the white patch on his left hindfoot.

"Where's your friend?"

She called out, "Kitty, kitty? Are you here?"

But the other tabby made no appearance.

"Well, at least you're here," she said to the cat. "I suppose the other one will come back soon, too. He always does."

The cat purred as she stroked his fur. She couldn't stop kissing his head. She was so grateful that he was there when she needed a friend.

"You won't believe what's happened," she said to the cat.

The kitty looked up at her and cocked his head to the side.

"Did you know that I've never been in love before? I wish I knew for sure what it felt like to be in love, kitty, because I think I'm feeling it."

She stroked the tabby, who nuzzled against her.

"The problem is, kitty, I think I'm falling for *two* men, and they're brothers."

The cat made a funny sound, like a cross between a hiss and a moan.

"Are you okay?" she asked him.

He licked her hand again. He seemed fine.

"Do you think that's even possible?" she asked him. "Is it possible to love two people at the same time?"

Still feeling cold from her wet hair, Ellie wished for a blanket. A soft golden quilt was suddenly draped across her, with the kitty underneath. He made his way out of the top of the cover and shook out his fur.

Ellie laughed. "Sorry, kitty."

Then she said, "But how could they do that to me? How could they trick me like that? If they really love me—and let's be honest: They only love me because their brother forced them to. There's no way they would have fallen in love with me naturally. But they do love me, so you would think they'd do everything in their power to make me feel safe."

Ellie stared at the fire as she stroked the tabby, who had climbed on top of the quilt and onto her lap.

"But maybe they *were* trying," she said after a few minutes. "Psyche had said weeks ago that the helm was the key to protecting me from the other gods. She said she'd make sure it was close to me."

Ellie began to piece together what had been going on. One of the brothers must always be nearby wearing the helm, ready to hide her at the first sign of trouble. This must have been going on for weeks. As she was getting to know the one brother, the other brother stood guard. More than likely, one of them was standing guard now.

"Deimos or Phobos? Which one of you is here?" she asked the seemingly empty room.

Deimos appeared with the helm in his hands. "Ellie, please let me explain."

"I'm counting on it." She held the orange tabby close and waited for Deimos to confirm what she'd already figured out.

"It was for your safety." He sat across from her on the gold ottoman.

"Was Phobos wearing the helm when you and I…"

Deimos nodded.

Ellie covered her mouth, even though he had given her the answer she'd expected.

"If I'd worn the helm during our dates, you wouldn't have been able to see me, unless we were touching the entire time. And even then, we would have been distracted and vulnerable. The helm provides invisibility, but sounds can still be heard. Someone could have thrown Poseidon's net over us and captured us before we knew it had happened."

Ellie sucked on her lips, processing Deimos's explanation.

"Phobos and I didn't want to waste any time helping you get to know us, hoping you'd fall for one of us. We agreed that this was the safest, most efficient…neither of us meant to get physical with you. I should have known Phobos was incapable of restraining himself. You can't imagine how hard it was to watch that night in the pool. I almost revealed myself to put a stop to it."

"Of course, I can imagine. It kills me, knowing I hurt you." Tears formed in her eyes.

Deimos knelt on the floor beside her. "Don't cry." He wiped her tears with his thumb. "Is it true what you said? Are you falling in love with us *both*?"

Ellie nodded as more tears spilled from her eyes. "I'm so sorry. I didn't think such a thing was possible. I mean, I've seen it happen on *The Bachelor* almost every season, but I didn't think it happened in *real* life."

Deimos squeezed her hand. "Don't apologize. Without Cupid's arrow in your heart, you could have gone the other way—you could have *despised* us both. At least there's still hope for *one* of us."

Ellie realized what Deimos was saying. She would eventually have to choose.

"You just need time," he said. "Time will tell which one of us you feel the most compatible with. We're so different, Ellie. You're bound to get along with one of us better than the other."

She couldn't imagine having to condemn one of them to a lifetime of heartache.

"No more tricks," she said. "I need you and Phobos to be honest with me, okay?"

Deimos sighed. "Did you hear that, Phobos?"

Ellie sat up and glanced around the room. Was Phobos there, too?

Suddenly the orange tabby leapt from her lap and morphed into the other twin.

Ellie's mouth fell open. "What the hell?"

When Apollo asked again why they were there, Cupid waited for his father to explain.

"It has to do with your visions," Ares finally said, "and the prophecies we received from Tiresias and the Fates."

"I thought as much."

Although he dreaded to tell the story again, Cupid relayed what he had done to his brothers and why he hoped to keep the mortal alive for as long as possible.

"A cure?" Apollo repeated. "I can tell you how to cure them."

Cupid sat up and lifted his chin. "I'm listening."

"Shoot them each with an arrow of hate."

"It's forbidden," Cupid reminded him.

"Not if they are without their powers," Apollo said.

"What are you getting at?" Ares asked.

"Ask Zeus to strip the twins of their powers," Apollo said.

"But he needs the support of the Olympian council to amass that kind of strength," Ares pointed out.

"I assure you, he would have it," Apollo said. "And when the twins are as weak as mortals, Cupid can drive an arrow of hate into each of their hearts as they're gazing upon the object of their desire. Then they will likely kill the girl and thwart the prophecy."

"Is that possible?" Cupid asked. "To thwart a prophecy?"

"My visions have been known to change," Apollo said. "Only the Fates know with certainty what the future holds."

"The Fates said the reckoning is coming, and that Ellie Beaufort is connected to it," Ares reminded him. "How could killing her thwart what the Fates have already deemed?"

"The reckoning is coming, you're right," Apollo said. "But my vision of the pillars of Mount Olympus crumbling—that's the part we may thwart. The consequences of the reckoning might change with Ellie Beaufort's speedy death."

"How can we convince Zeus and the council to strip my brothers of their powers?" Cupid asked Apollo.

Ares folded his hands. "Many of the Olympians rely on Phobos and Deimos to help carry out their purposes."

Apollo popped another grape into his mouth. "The twins are of no use to the other gods in their current condition, anyway."

"Good point," Ares said.

"We should go to Zeus with the truth," Apollo said.

"What would prevent him from striking Ellie dead at the first opportunity?" Cupid asked. "Before stripping Phobos and Deimos of their powers and allowing me to end their torment?"

"If Zeus can spare your brothers from an eternity of misery at very little cost to himself, he'll do it," Apollo said. "Have your brothers bring the girl to Mount Olympus, and we can get this over with today."

Cupid shook his head. "Phobos and Deimos would never hand her over in their current state."

Ares sighed. "We'll have to ambush them and take them by surprise."

"Then do it," Apollo said.

Ellie stood up from the green chaise lounge, thrust her hands in the pockets of the robe, and stared at the twins in shock.

"All this time?" she asked them. "You two have been the kitties?"

Before either god could reply, the fire in the hearth exploded, and then the flames extinguished, leaving behind a piece of parchment paper.

As Deimos went to pick it up, Phobos said, "It could be a trap. Better wear the helm."

Deimos set the helm on his head and disappeared. A moment later, the parchment vanished, too.

Ellie glanced at Phobos, whose formerly contrite expression had been replaced with concern. She opened her mouth to speak but was suddenly in the arms of Deimos, who then grabbed his brother.

A flash of bright light enveloped them, followed by an intense pressure. Ellie closed her eyes and opened them, finding she and the twins were no longer in her room in the castle, but in a mid-century modern apartment with a picture window overlooking a city.

"Where are we?" she asked them. "What's going on?"

"Deimos? What is it?" Phobos asked.

"A warning from Hecate," Deimos said, still wearing the helm. He'd linked elbows with them to keep them under its protection. "One of the muses overheard our father and Cupid talking with Apollo."

"Let me see that." Phobos took the parchment paper from his brother and read, "Urgent: Run! Terpsichore overheard Apollo advise Ares and Cupid to petition Zeus and the council to strip you of your powers. Cupid plans to shoot you with arrows of hate while you look upon Ellie Beaufort. They expect you will kill her and alter the prophecy. I repeat, run! –Hecate."

Ellie covered her mouth.

"This flat is the first place they'll look for us," Phobos said.

"I know," Deimos said. "I just wanted out of there. Where should we go from here?"

Phobos used his free hand to stuff the warning into his robe pocket. "I don't know. A different city? Or someplace remote, like the Himalayas?"

"There are more places to hide in a busy city," Deimos said. "I know just the one."

In the next instant, Phobos stood behind Ellie with one hand around her waist and the over her mouth. One of her elbows was still linked with Deimos's. Deimos held his finger to his lips and pointed.

She followed his finger to the other side of the flat, where Cupid, Ares, and one other god appeared out of thin air.

"I told you they knew better than to come here," Ares said.

Cupid flew about the room. "You forget they have the helm. Just because we can't see them doesn't mean they aren't here."

"Why on earth do they have the helm?" the third god asked.

"Aphrodite," Ares said. "She has her ways."

"If you're here, brothers," Cupid said. "I beg you to reveal yourselves. Try to think beyond the present moment to the eternity of misery you'll be condemned to once the mortal dies."

"We want to undo your brother's mistake," Ares added. "Nothing more."

"This is a waste of time," the third god said. "Hermes!"

A fourth god appeared in the room. Ellie gasped. All four gods turned in her direction. Deimos and Phobos lifted her in the air and hovered near the ceiling.

"You were right," Ares said to Cupid. "Listen to me, sons. We're only here to help."

"Hermes," the third god said. "Go to Poseidon and ask to borrow his golden net. If he won't part with it, ask him to bring it himself. Tell him it's urgent. The fate of Mount Olympus hangs in the balance."

"Yes, Lord Zeus."

The fourth god vanished.

Ellie and the twins were soon enveloped by a blinding light.

"They're attempting god-travel," Zeus said. "Catch their signatures!"

As soon as she'd closed her eyes, a pressure surrounded Ellie from all directions. When she opened them, she saw nothing but snow for miles. Another flash of light and pressure, and she was on a sandy beach. Another flash, and she was in a forest. Another flash, and she was in a what appeared to be a crowded casino. Dizzy and nauseous, Ellie leaned against the two gods for support, afraid to speak.

Deimos took her arm and led her through the crowd. Phobos, held her hand and took up the rear.

Once they were in the lobby of what Ellie realized was not just a casino but a fancy hotel, Deimos said, "I think we lost them."

"For now, anyway," Phobos said.

"Where are we?" Ellie asked.

Deimos smiled down at her. "Las Vegas."

Phobos, also grinning, added, "The city of sin."

Cupid followed the signatures left behind by god-travel to the island of Lesbo and lost the trail there.

"Found it," Zeus said. "Follow me."

They god-traveled to Brazil, to the thickest part of the Amazon rain-forest.

"Clever boys," Ares said. "They knew the humidity would erase their tracks."

"What do we do now?" Cupid asked.

"Hecate can perform a location spell," Zeus said. "Let's return to Mount Olympus and get her working on it immediately."

They rode together in Zeus's chariot back to the east, to the gates of Mount Olympus, where the seasons opened the gates and let them in. In the garage, Cupid unbridled the horses and fed them some hay before joining the others in the great hall, where Psyche was waiting for him.

Telepathically, she asked Cupid, *What have you done?*

I'm saving Mount Olympus, he replied as he waited for Zeus to return with Hecate from Demeter's chambers.

You don't know that, Psyche said. *You don't know that Ellie's death will change anything.*

Apollo thinks there's a chance.

She's innocent. She doesn't deserve this. Gods are supposed to make sacrifices for mortals, not the other way around.

Although not all the gods shared Psyche's sentiment, Cupid did. He didn't want Ellie Beaufort to die. But he felt it was a concession he'd have to make to save his brothers.

Zeus returned from Demeter's room alone.

To Psyche, Cupid said, *Let's talk later.*

"Hecate needs to gather a few items first," Zeus said. "Then she will begin."

CHAPTER FIFTEEN

Vegas

"Why are you using a key card?" Ellie asked Deimos as he pressed the card to the door of the penthouse suite of the casino hotel. "Can't we just pop in?"

"We need to avoid god-travel." Deimos opened the door. "It leaves a residue behind that can be tracked by other gods."

"Oh."

"Welcome to your new hideout," Phobos said to Ellie.

Ellie tightened the belt on her robe and looked around the suite. Whereas the castle had possessed an old-world charm, and the London flat had had a mid-century modern flare, the penthouse suite had a contemporary vibe with white walls, chrome and glass finishes, and sleek white furniture, including a sectional with a chaise on one side and a matching square ottoman in the center, and a flat-screen television along the opposite wall. Behind the sectional were a kitchen and dining area. Along with a gorgeous bouquet of red roses, the glass dining table held a silver tray with long-stem glassware and an ice bucket with a bottle of champagne. Although she'd stayed in hotels when her softball team played in other cities and states, she'd never stayed in one this fancy.

Deimos removed the helm and closed the door behind them.

Phobos jerked his thumb toward the helm. "Shouldn't one of us keep that on?"

"We did a good job of losing them." Deimos handed the helm to Phobos. "But you can wear it, if you want. It's not the most comfortable headwear."

"Or the most fashionable," Phobos said. "How long do you think we have before anyone tracks us here?"

Deimos collapsed on one end of the white sectional. "Only Hecate has the ability to locate us without a search party. And she's on our side, it seems."

"She could be forced, against her will," Phobos said. "Zeus has ways of getting information when he wants it."

Deimos heaved a heavy sigh. "You're right. We need to be ready for the unexpected."

Phobos cocked his head to the side. "Doesn't expecting the unexpected make the unexpected expected?"

Ellie realized he was trying to be funny, to put her at ease, but she was tired and frightened and in no mood to laugh. "What do we do now?"

"I vote for Blackjack," Phobos said. "But Deimos prefers the slots."

"You aren't serious," Ellie said.

"Dead serious," Phobos said. "He's lost enough money on slot machines to feed several small countries."

Ellie glanced through a set of sliding glass doors leading to a balcony. Dusk was just beginning to settle over the Las Vegas strip below. When she remembered that it was well past midnight in Greece, she understood why, along with the fear and confusion, she was so very sleepy.

Phobos flew to her side and pulled the drapes closed around the glass doors. "Don't stand near the windows. You could be seen."

Phobos flew around closing the drapes on the other windows, too.

Ellie turned away, still not sure if she should be angry with the twins or grateful.

"How are you holding up, Ellie?" Deimos asked from the sectional. "You look exhausted."

She yawned and thrust her hands into the pockets of the robe. "I need to pee and go to bed. Maybe when I wake up, you can explain to me what the hell is going on. I'm too tired to hear it right now." She pointed to one of two bedrooms off the living room. "I'll take this one."

"We need to stay together," Deimos said to Phobos as Ellie left the room. "It's not just her they're after."

Sitting alone in the bathroom, Ellie reflected on what had happened. It was still so hard to believe. Yet this toilet felt real, and this tissue. This robe felt real. She flushed and washed her hands. This sink and vanity felt real. In the mirror, she looked dead-dog tired. That was definitely real.

At least she was back in America in a city she'd heard of and not on the top of a steep mountaintop.

Ellie pulled back the plush white comforter and soft sheets on the king-size bed and crawled beneath them. She had just slipped the robe off from underneath the covers when the twins entered and sat on chairs on either side of the bed.

"What are you doing?" she asked them.

"We have to stick together," Deimos said. "In case we need to use the helm."

"Are you just going to sit there and watch me sleep?" she asked them.

"Got any better ideas?" Phobos asked with a playful grin.

"Would it make you feel better if one of us took our cat form while the other wore the helm?" Deimos offered.

"I do miss those kitties," Ellie said, "but now it's just weird."

"Duly noted," Phobos said, looking hurt.

Ellie closed her eyes. "Can you at least turn on the TV?"

One of the twins must have found the remote, because Ellie heard what sounded like a baseball game playing on the television perched on a dresser across from the bed. She opened her eyes. The Red Sox were playing the Astros, and the Red Sox were ahead by one.

"Can you put it on something boring? Like golf?" she asked.

Phobos snapped his fingers. Apparently, gods didn't need remotes. "This looks interesting."

It was a sex scene. A woman lay naked on her back as a man ravished her breasts.

Ellie closed her eyes and rolled over. "Watch what you want."

But the memory of being in the pool with Phobos as he cupped her breasts aroused her. She peeked at the gods, who were still watching the sex scene. Phobos glanced at her and caught her looking at him.

In a flash, he was lying on top of the covers beside her on the bed. He stroked her cheek. "I'm sorry, brother. I can't stand it. I need to touch her."

Deimos appeared on the other side of Ellie. He propped his head with his elbow and gently stroked Ellie's arm. "Is this okay, Ellie? Or does it make you feel uncomfortable?"

She wanted to say, "Are you kidding? I'm in heaven." But, instead, she said, "It feels nice."

"Good." Phobos kissed her forehead. "Get some rest now, dear Ellie."

"We'll keep you safe." Deimos kissed her shoulder.

Ellie lay there, enjoying the sensation of being caressed by the two warm bodies beside her. She felt less afraid and panicky lying between them, but those feelings were quickly replaced by anticipation. She couldn't sleep because she kept expecting one, or both, of them to kiss her.

Ellie eventually fell asleep, however, because, sometime later, she awoke from an amazing dream in which Phobos and Deimos had taken turns making love to her while the other twin watched.

She was surprised to find both gods sound asleep on either side of her. So much for keeping her safe.

"Good morning," Deimos said as he opened his eyes.

"Sleep well?" she half-teased.

Phobos stretched. "We weren't asleep. Just lying here with our eyes closed, listening."

"And waiting," Deimos added.

"Listening to what?" Ellie asked.

Phobos pulled his pillow from beneath his head and hit her with it. "Listening to you sleep."

"Hey!" she said, hitting him back with the pillow. "I can't help it, you know."

"It was nice when we were cats," Deimos said, "but it's pure misery as men."

"It's been very miserable," Phobos agreed.

"The worst kind of torture," Deimos added. "Not being able to do all the things I'd like to do to you."

"Stop, Deimos," Phobos said. "You're making it worse."

Ellie laughed, ignoring the deep blush that warmed her cheeks. "What time is it?"

"Approaching midnight, Las Vegas time," Deimos said.

"Let's whip on some clothes and play the slots," Phobos suggested as he flew off the bed. "We need a distraction."

By the time he'd landed on his feet, he was wearing jeans, boots, and a forest-green button-down shirt.

"I thought you wanted to play Blackjack?" Ellie asked Phobos as she admired his new look.

"We'll have the helm." Deimos jumped out of bed with a fresh set of clothes on, too. He wore black trousers with a baby blue shirt and a paisley tie—an equally hot though different look than his brother's.

"The slots will be less conspicuous," Phobos explained. "If cards moved by invisible hands at the Blackjack table, you can bet they'd be noticed."

"Come here, and I'll help you dress," Deimos offered.

Phobos lifted a warning finger. "I wouldn't trust his taste."

Ellie reached over the side of the bed and grabbed her white robe. "I know you can see through this thing, but I feel less vulnerable wearing it."

Once she had the belt securely tied around her waist, Ellie climbed from the bed and stood between the two gods. "If we're using the helm, why do clothes matter?"

"I like the way she thinks," Phobos said with a grin. "Let's get nakie."

"That's not what I meant."

Deimos crossed his arms and shook his head while giving his brother a look of disapproval. "It's best to be prepared for anything."

Deimos snapped his fingers. Ellie's robe was replaced by a white silky, button-down blouse—with the top few buttons undone. She wore gray trousers and a silver belt and black patent leather shoes with a short heel. Gazing at her reflection in the mirror on the back of the bedroom door, Ellie noticed she wore no bra with a see-through top.

"Seriously?" she asked.

"My sentiments exactly," Phobos said.

He snapped his fingers, and suddenly she was wearing tight-fitting jeans, high-heeled boots, and a red halter top with a low back. Again, she was wearing no bra.

"I'm not your Barbie doll," she said. "Just put me in something comfortable. Please?"

Before Deimos could say anything, Phobos said, "Let me, brother."

Phobos snapped his fingers. The jeans became loose-fitting, the boots shorter-heeled, and the top long-sleeved. She also was—finally—wearing a bra.

"Better," she said. "Let's go."

Phobos wore the helm. Ellie took the arm of each twin, and they escorted her to the casino on the bottom floor.

On the way down in the otherwise empty elevator, Deimos reminded her not to lose contact with Phobos. He also said she shouldn't speak, except when they were in the crowd, where no one would notice.

A few of Ellie's teammates had been to Vegas, and she'd envied their stories of hitting jackpots—though they always came back with less money than they had when they left. Ellie was sure that if she were to hit it big, she would stop while she was ahead.

For the first half hour, Ellie watched Deimos play as he explained to her how to use the voucher, how to increase bets, and other strategies, which varied from machine to machine. Each time he showed her something new, she'd say, "Why thank you, Professor Deimos."

While Deimos played, Phobos provided her with an endless supply of drinks and snacks, which he stole from the bar at long distance. He speculated that some poor waiter or bartender would likely be blamed for the missing inventory, so he sent lots of extra cash to the tip jars.

Three drinks in, it was finally Ellie's turn to play. Deimos guided her as she pushed buttons and eagerly watched the screen. She felt giddy and slightly drunk.

"Look at that!" Deimos cried when her credit went from $55 to $175.

"Should I stop while I'm ahead?" she asked.

Phobos scoffed. "What's the fun in that?"

"It's too early in the night to stop now," Deimos said. "Keep going."

Ellie was excited as she continued to push buttons. "Come on, Lady Luck," she muttered.

"Wait," Phobos grabbed her arm. "Did you just pray?"

"Huh?"

"She prayed to Lady Luck," Deimos said. "I heard it too. We need to get out of here."

"It's just a figure of speech," Ellie said. "I don't want to leave. I'm winning."

"Maybe Tyche doesn't know who Ellie is," Phobos said.

"By now, everyone knows," Deimos said.

Phobos nodded. "You're probably right. Zeus has probably held a council meeting and planted spies all over the globe."

"We need to god-travel out before someone's on our tail," Deimos said.

"Too late," Phobos said, nodding his head to their right.

"I don't see anything," Ellie said.

"Zeus is here with Cupid and Ares," Deimos explained. "Don't talk and follow me."

Arm in arm, Deimos led them through the crowded casino and out into the cool night.

"I have an idea." Phobos positioned himself in front of Ellie, placing her hands on his shoulders. "Don't let go, Ellie. Deimos, help me carry her to Selene's chariot. We'll hitch a ride to the other side of the world."

"That's actually a good idea, Phobos," Deimos said.

"Why, thank you, brother."

Sandwiched in between the two gods, Ellie tried not to scream as they flew from the ground and up into the night sky. When they passed a layer of clouds, her stomach dropped, and her ears popped. She felt dizzy and delirious as she glanced at the ground, barely perceptible from this height.

"Are you okay?" Deimos whispered in her ear.

His warmth breath made her shiver.

Deimos felt it and chuckled. "Ellie?"

"I'm trying not to scream," she finally said.

"We're nearly there," Phobos said from upfront. "Hang on."

In the distance, Ellie saw the moon, bright and glorious.

"You may need to close your eyes," Deimos whispered.

"No more talking," Phobos scolded. "Selene will hear."

Ellie kept her eyes open for as long as she could stand it, squinting against the brilliant moonlight. She could just make out a silver chariot and two silver horses with iridescent manes. A goddess with a long flowing luminous robe and silver and iridescent hair was their driver. But that was all Ellie could see before the light nearly blinded her.

Cupid had been ecstatic when his half-sister, Tyche, had reported contact with Ellie Beaufort at a Casino in Las Vegas amid the countless others begging for her favor. The mortals called her "Lady Luck," and although Nemesis was her constant companion, leveling out the fortune as fast as Tyche arbitrarily gave it, enough people came out ahead to guarantee Tyche's popularity.

Cupid and his father and grandfather dispatched to Vegas immediately in Zeus's chariot and met Tyche on a rooftop. Tyche pointed in the direction from which she'd heard the mortal's prayer, and damn if it wasn't one of the most crowded casinos on the strip.

Invisible to mortals, the three gods scoured the establishment for any sign of Phobos and Deimos and their mortal captive, along with any signatures left behind by god-travel.

When they found nothing, Zeus was so enraged, that he flew to the rooftop and chewed out Tyche for wasting their time. Brought to tears, Tyche swore her information was good.

"You just weren't fast enough," she said, which only infuriated Zeus more.

Cupid didn't need the prophetic powers of Apollo to know that, for the rest of the night—if not the next—no one playing on the Vegas strip would hit a jackpot of any significance.

CHAPTER SIXTEEN

Selene

The beams of the moon goddess were warm against Ellie's skin, and their brilliance was visible from behind closed lids. Ellie clung to Phobos and Deimos from where she sat between them on the silver chariot as they rode across the sky. She wished she could see what she imagined was a spectacular sight.

In her mind, she thought, *Oh, Selene, I wish I could see how beautiful you are.*

At that moment, Ellie heard a woman say, "Who's there?"

The words had barely been uttered when Deimos was violently shoved against Ellie, who, in turn, fell against Phobos, from whose head the helm must have toppled, for he shouted, "The helm!"

Ellie tried to look but was blinded as the chariot swerved and the goddess said, "Well, well. What do we have here?"

"Please, let us explain," Deimos said.

The brilliance faded against Ellie's lids and skin. She shivered in the cold night until Deimos and Phobos radiated heat to warm her.

"You can look at me now, mortal," the goddess said.

Ellie opened her eyes to find Selene standing before her, and the goddess was holding the helm. Iridescent ropes, the same color as the goddess's hair, bound Ellie and the twins to the chariot.

Selene's luminous hair and robe flew about her in the wind. Her silver eyes looked down at Ellie, not with anger or hatred, but with curiosity.

"We meant you no harm," Deimos said.

"Unless," Phobos said with a grin, "you consider hitching a free ride harmful to you."

Selene lifted the powerful object in her hands. "What business do you have with this helm?"

Deimos confessed everything to the moon goddess, which surprised Ellie, who thought it would have been safer to lie. Wouldn't the goddess take them directly to Mount Olympus?

While Selene listened, her horses continued to pull the chariot across the sky. They probably knew this route, since they'd been taking it every day for centuries. Ellie dared to look over the side at the darkness below. Occasionally she'd recognize the shadow of a cloud, but everything else was pitch black.

When Deimos had finished recounting all that had happened, including Zeus's desire to strip him and his brother of their powers so Cupid could shoot them with arrows of hate, driving them to kill Ellie, Selene said, "Try to run, and you'll be sorry. I won't hand you over to Zeus, but I will keep you prisoner until I learn if your story checks out."

"You may as well hand us over, if you're going to ask questions," Phobos said. "The result will be the same."

"Selene, I beg you," Deimos said. "If you talk to anyone, please speak with Hecate, and make sure you're not overheard. Everyone else is out to get us."

"Hecate is a trusted friend," Selene said. "I'll wear this helm and seek her out. If her story aligns with yours, I'll release you."

Ellie didn't know how much time had passed before the chariot began to descend toward a mountaintop above the clouds. It slowed as it entered the mouth of a cavern before coming to a full stop. Although the gods had dimmed themselves for Ellie's sake, they were still bright enough to illuminate the entirety of the large cave, which was furnished as nicely as any house, including a fountain and, beyond it, a bed. Ellie was surprised to see someone already in the bed sleeping.

"That's my lover," Selene explained. "Don't disturb him. If I learn he was awakened in my absence, I'll take you to Zeus myself."

"What if he wakes up on his own?" Ellie asked, suddenly not so sure of the goddess's benevolence.

"He won't," came her curt reply.

Selene unbridled her horses and gave them hay and water. Then she released the iridescent ropes binding Ellie and the twins to the chariot.

"You can make yourselves comfortable on the furniture," the moon goddess said. "You won't be able to leave this cave without sounding my alarm. It can be heard even as far as Mount Olympus."

"Please tell me you have Netflix," Phobos said with a grin.

Without another word, Selene vanished.

"We need to have a talk," Deimos said when they were alone in the cave, save for the sleeping lover. "I'm sorry we didn't explain this to you more clearly."

Phobos flew to one of the couches and made himself comfortable. "I don't think she's aware she's doing it. Mortals are like that."

"Like what?" Ellie asked.

Phobos patted the cushion beside him. "Come have a seat and Professor Deimos will explain, I'm sure."

Deimos took Ellie's hand and led her across the room and sat her next to Phobos. Then he knelt on the floor in front of her to warm her legs.

Phobos wrapped an arm around her shoulders, and heat radiated from the two gods throughout her entire body.

"Let's have a fire, too," Phobos said just before flames illuminated the hearth on the other side of the cave.

"Are you sure that won't wake up that guy?" Ellie asked.

"I'm sure," Phobos said. "He doesn't even wake up for sex."

Ellie's brows lifted. "What?"

Deimos hugged her legs. "Let's stay on track, shall we? This is important, Ellie. You mustn't pray. Understand?"

"Huh?" Ellie wasn't sure why she was getting this lecture. "I never pray. I'm not a religious person."

"See?" Phobos said. "Told ya. Mortals are just like that."

"Like what?" Ellie asked again.

"You pray without realizing it," Phobos replied. "It's like you're wired to. Maybe Prometheus made you that way."

"Who's Prometheus?" she asked.

"I'll tell you about him another time," Deimos said. "The point is you need to be aware of your thoughts. Like Phobos said, you're praying without even realizing it."

"I am?"

"That's how Cupid and the others found us in Vegas," Deimos explained. "You prayed to Tyche, also known as Lady Luck."

Ellie lifted her head and said, "Oh. Oh my gosh."

"Did you pray to Selene in the chariot?" Deimos asked. "Because I can't figure out how else she sensed our presence."

Ellie tried to recall. "I don't think so. I remember wishing I could see her."

Phobos squeezed her shoulder. "Bet you didn't know you told me I looked delicious."

Ellie's cheeks burned. "When did I say that?"

"You prayed it to me, over our first dinner date," Phobos said. "When we were alone."

"And the night before that," Deimos said, "you begged me to kiss you."

"I did not!"

"And you've done so many times since," Deimos added.

"Okay, that's enough," Phobos said. "I think she gets the point."

Ellie jumped to her feet and held her cheeks. "It's like you can read my mind."

"Only when you address us in your thoughts." Deimos stood up and took her hand, leading her to stand with him by the fire. "That's the difference between thought and prayer: prayers are thoughts that are addressed to a specific person."

"Just think about people in third person," Phobos said. "So instead of thinking, 'Phobos, you're so hot,' you should think, 'That Phobos, he's hot.'"

"That's what happened with Selene!" she realized suddenly.

"You told her she was hot?" Phobos asked with his head cocked to the side. "Oh, that *is* hot."

"I told her I wished I could see how beautiful she was."

"That's why she was so easy on us," Deimos said. "You flattered her."

"You consider this easy on us?" Ellie asked.

"It could have been much worse," Phobos said.

"I nearly ruined everything." Ellie fought back tears. "Me and my dumb head."

Deimos took her in his arms and smoothed her hair from her eyes. "Don't talk like that."

She wrapped her arms around his neck and allowed him to comfort her as tears spilled down her cheeks. It felt so good to be in his arms— warm and safe. From the corner of her eye, she saw Phobos watching them. She held her hand out to him and prayed, *Come here, Phobos.*

He embraced her from behind and kissed the back of her head. "It's going to be okay," he whispered in her ear, sending shivers down her spine.

Whether it was the fear of imminent death or the excitement of being held by two sexy gods who happened to be in love with her, Ellie wanted to kiss them. She couldn't dare hurt one by choosing the other; besides, she was in love with them both. The more time she spent with them, the more certain she felt. Maybe things would have been different in the real world if she had met them on campus and they hadn't been such interesting and powerful beings. But right now, she felt that she loved them, and she needed them.

Since it was too hard to say it out loud, she prayed to them:

Phobos and Deimos, I want to kiss you—both of you. Is that weird?

"I'll take a kiss from you however I can get it," Phobos said breathlessly as he spun her around.

He slipped his arms around her waist and crushed her against him as his mouth pressed hard against hers. He pulled on her lips with his, and this time, she bit back, only further enflaming his passion—and hers.

"My turn," Deimos said.

He waited for her to come to him before he held her face and looked into her eyes.

"You're so beautiful," he whispered as he gently touched his lips to hers.

His slow, lingering kisses aroused her just as deeply as the violent kisses from his brother. Deimos offered her his tongue, and she accepted it before offering him hers. He moaned and encircled her waist, lifting her off the ground before setting her down again.

"I can't stop myself," she heard Phobos say from behind her just before he slipped his hands beneath her arms and cupped her breasts.

Ellie gasped against Deimos's kisses as she pressed against Phobos's hands. Deimos caressed her cheek, stroked her hair, and then licked her ear, while Phobos squeezed her breast with one hand and her bottom with the other. Wet between her legs, Ellie felt an urgent need to rub herself against Deimos's thigh.

"You boys don't waste any time, do you?" Selene said from the mouth of the cave.

The kissing and caressing came to a halt as all three looked at Selene with varying degrees of embarrassment and humiliation.

"Did you speak with Hecate?" Deimos asked.

"I did. Your story checks out."

"Where's the helm?" Phobos asked.

"I returned it to Hades."

"You what?" Deimos and Phobos said simultaneously.

"I owed him a favor," Selene said. "Now we're even."

Phobos sighed. "This is not good."

"Don't worry," Selene said. "I handed it over without explanation."

"I'm surprised the cavalry isn't already here," Phobos said.

"I have a message from Hecate," Selene said. "She wants you to hide in the forest on Circe's Island and wait for her there."

"Circe's island?" Phobos repeated.

"Did she say why?" Deimos asked.

"She knows how to save the mortal's life," Selene said. "But Hecate requires time to gather what she needs, and Circe's Island is the last place anyone would think to look for you."

"How do we know we can trust Hecate?" Ellie asked Phobos and Deimos.

"She helped us once before," Deimos pointed out.

"We're short on options," Phobos said, taking Ellie's hand.

"Wait," Deimos said to Phobos. "No god-travel. If Zeus and the others track us here, they might pick up our signatures."

"But it's too dangerous to fly all the way to Circe's Island without the helm," Phobos said.

"You could always catch a ride with my brother," Selene suggested. "He'll be coming by in his golden cup any minute now."

Ellie turned to Deimos. "Who's her brother?"

"Helios," he said. "The sun god."

Phobos shook his head. "I don't know, Deimos. The more people who know a secret, the less likely it is to stay a secret."

Selene laughed. "Who would Helios tell? He has no love for Zeus or for Mount Olympus."

"She has a point," Deimos said.

"But Circe is his daughter," Phobos said. "Won't he wonder why we're going to her island?"

"I can see his horses now," Selene said from where she stood at the mouth of the cave. "It's now or never."

Deimos took Ellie's hand. "Let's go."

The three stood hand in hand at the edge of Selene's cave as Helios's chariot approached. Ellie kept her eyes closed, but this did little to keep the bright rays from nearly blinding her. The heat, too, would not have been tolerable had the two gods beside her not shielded her from it.

Ellie overheard Deimos ask if they could have a ride as far as the Ionian Sea.

"Hop in," Ellie heard the sun god say.

One of the twins picked her up—she could tell it was Phobos, perhaps by his scent—and carried her into the chariot. Once they were settled and introductions were made, Deimos explained that Helios's vehicle was often called a golden cup because, unlike the more popular box-like models, it was round, like a bowl, with a bench seat all around it.

After a bit of silence, Helios said, "I won't ask who you're running from if you won't mention you were here."

"Deal," Phobos said.

CHAPTER SEVENTEEN

Circe's Island

Ellie awoke with her face in Deimos's chest, and she'd nearly blinded herself before remembering to shut her eyes against the harsh rays of Helios.

Deimos held her tight and whispered, "We're nearly there."

"Where are we now?" Ellie asked.

Before he could answer, Ellie was startled by the voice of a fifth person in the chariot—a female.

"Oh, my," the newcomer said. "I didn't realize you had passengers. Hello, Phobos. Hello, Deimos. Who's your mortal friend?"

"Rhode?" Helios said. "Oh, yes!"

"Don't tell me you forgot about our appointment this afternoon," the newcomer scolded.

"My memory isn't what it used to be," Helios replied. "But don't, fret, dear. I'll be rid of my guests in thirty minutes, tops."

"I don't think I want to wait around for you," Rhode said. "I have things to do."

"How disappointing," the sun god said. "Are you sure you can't be persuaded to stay? I promise to make it worth your while."

Ellie didn't have to open her eyes to see that she and the twins had interfered with a sexually charged rendezvous.

"Where are you taking them?" Rhode asked.

"The Ionian Sea," Helios replied. "We're almost there."

"I'll meet you here again tomorrow," Rhode said. "But, if you forget, I'll never visit you at work again. Goodbye."

Helios sighed. "You try to do a good deed, and what do you get?"

"Sorry, Helios," Deimos said. "We didn't mean to ruin your day."

"Look on the bright side—ha! Get it? The bright side?" Phobos slapped his knee. "Like there's any other side to Helios!"

Deimos groaned. "Please excuse my brother."

"But there is a *brighter* side." Phobos grinned. "You can now look forward to tomorrow's makeup sex, which is the best kind, wouldn't you agree?"

"You make a valid argument," Helios said with a laugh.

Ellie frowned, wondering how much makeup sex Phobos had had. She wrapped her arms more tightly around Deimos, keeping her face in his chest, and stewed.

After a while, Helios said, "We've reached the Ionian Sea. Isn't this where you wanted off?"

"Yes," Deimos said. "Thank you. Ready?"

This time it was Deimos who whisked her up in his arms and carried her through the air. Once again, her stomach dropped, and her ears popped. Even after they were far enough away that the light from Helios wasn't glaring at her through her eyelids, she kept her eyes closed, face buried in Deimos's neck.

To distract herself from what felt like a free fall from thousands of miles in the sky, she asked Deimos, "Who's Rhode?"

"Poseidon's daughter and Helios's wife."

"Poseidon's daughter?" she repeated.

"One of the sea nymphs that Phobos used to chase around."

"Even though she's married?" Ellie asked.

"I can hear you, Deimos," Phobos said. "If we're going to start sharing stories about the past…"

"Look, there it is," Deimos said. "Circe's island. Come on."

Ellie opened her eyes, but the island was too far away to see with mortal eyes, so she closed them again. Before long, Deimos slowed down and landed with her among twisted, leaning trees. Phobos landed beside them.

"Ugh. What's that smell?" Ellie asked as she glanced around. "And what's wrong with these trees?"

"Circe's noxious fumes, from her chimney," Deimos explained, as he set her on her feet. "They've corrupted the forest and everything in it, so stay close."

"You mean I'm breathing poison?" she asked as she covered her mouth with the top of her shirt.

"Calm down, Ellie," Phobos said. "You'll breathe in less of it if you don't speak."

Is that another way of asking me to shut up? Ellie wondered.

Phobos grinned, as if he'd heard her, and Ellie wondered if she'd confused a thought with a prayer again.

"Let's find a comfortable spot to wait for Hecate," Deimos said. "Come on."

They marched through the brush, with Deimos in the lead, until they came upon a trail.

"I can't remember which way leads to Circe's house, can you?" Deimos asked his brother.

Phobos pointed to their left. "That way." Then he looked to their right. "No, that way."

"Let's go left. It's downhill," Deimos said. "Besides, first impressions are usually right. If we come to the witch's clearing, we'll turn back and go the other way."

"Sound plan, brother. Lead the way, and I'll take up the rear. The view is better back here."

Still hurt by the comment about makeup sex, Ellie rolled her eyes at Phobos before turning to follow Deimos.

"What?" Phobos asked.

Ellie ignored him, opting to study the twisted trees they passed along the way. She held the top of her shirt over her mouth, to avoid the poisonous fumes. She followed Deimos closely, because the rays of the sun god barely penetrated the thick canopy of leaves overhead, and, although it was early morning, the forest was dark.

"Why are we hiking when we could fly?" Ellie asked Deimos.

"We're less conspicuous this way," Deimos replied. "We need to stay low to the ground."

Not fifteen minutes had passed when they reached a clearing. From the edge of the woods, the witch's house looked massive and angular beneath the bright rays of the sun. The house had a modern flare with a triangular chimney, stone walls, and lots of windows. Large billowing puffs of white smoke rose from the chimney and formed a blanket over the island. Ellie stifled a cough.

"Turn back," Deimos said. "And this time, I get the rear."

Ellie flashed Deimos a smile before turning to follow Phobos.

Phobos arched a brow. "Did I say something to offend you?"

Ellie wasn't expecting him to confront her. She was used to people ignoring her when she moped.

"I'm just wondering how much makeup sex you've had."

Phobos grinned, which made Ellie mad.

"Just forget it and lead the way," she said.

Phobos did as she asked, but she could see he was pleased with himself. She decided to relax and enjoy the view, since it was nice for Ellie in either direction.

When the slope of the trail became steep, Phobos turned back to her and asked, "Want a lift?"

Without answering, she jumped onto him, piggy-back style, holding onto his broad shoulders. He pushed her bottom to move her higher up and held her legs around his trunk. As he continued forward, Ellie had the unexpected pleasure of her crotch bouncing against his back. She nestled her face into the nape of his neck, linked her hands across his chest, and allowed her breasts to bounce against him, too.

She wouldn't mind if the trail went on forever, though she doubted it would take her long to cum.

After a while, she worried Phobos would notice how damp she'd become between her legs. On the other hand, why hide it from him? Surely, he'd love to know. She squeezed him between her thighs and sighed against his nape.

I want you so bad, she prayed to Phobos.

He clasped her hands near his throat and gave them a squeeze.

She hadn't forgotten about Deimos. She glanced back at him, and though he smiled back at her and tried to hide his jealousy, she could see he wished he was in his brother's place.

Touch me, Deimos, she prayed while she looked back at him.

His eyes widened with surprise. As she turned to lay her cheek against Phobos's nape, she was pleased when Deimos came up behind her and pressed his hand along her bottom, on the outside of her jeans, right down to the sweet spot, already wet with anticipation.

Phobos stopped in his tracks, and Deimos bumped into them.

"Look at this," Phobos said.

Ellie lifted her head. They'd stopped before a wide, hollowed-out tree. The tree was as wide as a minivan and nearly as deep, and it was the tallest in the forest. Through the opening, Ellie could see a bed—not of leaves, but of blankets and pillows.

"Maybe Hecate put this here for us, so we could wait for her in comfort," Deimos said. "Let's check it out."

Phobos released Ellie's legs, and she slid down his back, enjoying the feeling of her breasts mashed against him before her feet hit the ground. It took her a second to regain her balance. The place between her legs still ached to be touched.

She followed the twins through the small opening and into the hollowed-out tree. There was nothing but darkness above them, until the light from Deimos radiated up and showed that the tree was hollow for another six feet. Along with the light from the twins, a few rays from the sun god sifted through the canopy and dimly lit the bed.

"It's a mattress stuffed with feathers," Phobos said as he made himself comfortable. "Ah. Thank you, Hecate."

Deimos touched Ellie's arm. "You'll be safe here while we wait. Let's lie down and rest."

Suddenly feeling shy and awkward, Ellie crawled onto the bed beside Phobos. Deimos laid on his stomach on the other side of her and looked down at her.

"How do you feel?" he asked.

I think you know, she prayed.

His smile cracked his face in two.

"What's so funny?" Phobos asked.

Not wanting to leave him out, and too shy to say it out loud, Ellie prayed: *I got so turned on rubbing against your back that I asked Deimos to touch me, and he did.*

"Then it's my turn to touch you," Phobos said in his husky, less playful tone.

Ellie gasped when Phobos pinched her between the legs, kneading her flesh through her jeans with his fingers. It was a delightful combination of pleasure and pain that had her dying for more.

She closed her eyes. "Don't stop."

While Phobos rubbed her in just the right spot between her legs, Deimos moved his hands beneath the bottom of her shirt. He tugged at her bra and made it disappear. Then he massaged each breast and pinched her nipples, causing her body to writhe in ecstasy.

She opened her eyes to find both gods watching her with looks of lustful passion on their faces. She turned to Deimos and prayed to him to kiss her.

His lips moved softly against hers, caressing her mouth and tongue. Tears of joy sprang from her eyes, and she moaned with delight as his tongue gently explored her mouth.

Then she turned to Phobos and prayed to him to kiss her.

In her ear, he whispered, "You saved the best for last."

Phobos tugged at her ear with his lips before pressing his mouth hard against hers. He sucked on bottom lip and took it between his teeth. Then he moved his mouth down her throat and gently bit her neck. All the while his fingers continued to rub her in the right spot, bringing her to the brink of orgasm.

"I think I'm going to explode," she whispered as she closed her eyes and threw back her head. "Oh, my gods, I'm exploding."

Her body pulsed beneath Phobos's hand in an explosion of pleasure. Although Ellie had experimented on her own, she'd never felt an orgasm so deep.

When the pulsing came to an end and a wave of euphoria swept through her body, she opened her eyes. Deimos had buried his face in her neck. Phobos looked down at her and smiled.

She mouthed, "Thank you" to Phobos, who gave her a nod before falling back on the bed beside her.

Deimos kissed her neck and whispered, "I love you." Then he pulled her backside into him and spooned her.

She held Deimos's hand with her bottom hand and reached her free arm across Phobos's broad chest. Phobos clasped her hand in his and closed his eyes. She felt the beat of his heart.

"I feel as if I've died and gone to heaven," she whispered.

"It makes me happy to hear that," Deimos whispered in her ear. "Though, technically, it's called the Elysian Fields."

"Thank you, Professor," Phobos muttered.

"Are you sure you're okay with this?" she asked them.

Deimos said, "I'd rather have you like this than not at all."

Phobos turned to face her. He stroked her cheek and then ran his thumb across her bottom lip. He looked into her eyes and said, "I feel the same way. I'd rather share you than make you choose and risk losing."

Ellie took a deep breath and let it out slowly. "I wish this was real."

"What do you mean?" Phobos asked. "Of course, this is real."

"I assure you this isn't a dream," Deimos said gently into her ear.

"But you only love me because Cupid forced you to. If it weren't for his arrows, I'd be nothing to you."

"That's not true," Deimos said, pulling her in closer against him.

"First of all," Phobos began, "an arrow of Eros only works on those who already possess the potential to fall in love."

"Really?" she asked, wiping a tear from the corner of her eye.

Phobos nodded.

"He's right," Deimos said.

"And second of all," Phobos continued, "if Cupid could find a way to remove this arrow, my feelings for you wouldn't change."

"You don't know that," she said.

"Sure, I do," Phobos said.

"We've gotten to know how incredible you are," Deimos said. "There's no going back."

"But I'm not incredible—just average."

Deimos squeezed her hand. "You're kind and compassionate."

"And fun and sexy," Phobos added, stroking her hair.

"Inquisitive, intelligent, and strong," Deimos said.

"You let us into your heart," Phobos said. "No one's ever done that—at least, not to me."

"Nor me," Deimos said.

"I really must have died," Ellie said as more tears filled her eyes. "And yet, I did nothing to deserve this heaven—or whatever you call it."

Phobos wiped her tears with his thumb. "Don't cry."

Deimos buried his face in the back of Ellie's hair. "Dear, sweet, Ellie."

CHAPTER EIGHTEEN

Capture

Cupid stood beside his father's throne in the great hall of Mount Olympus. His father sat with his chin in his hand, listening to Poseidon, god of the sea, address the council. All the Olympians were there, save Hades.

"According to Rhode," Poseidon was saying, "they could be anywhere in the Ionian Sea. I'd bet my fastest mare that they've gone to the old crab and his wife to strike up an alliance."

"Phorcys would like nothing more than to see Mount Olympus crumble," Zeus agreed.

Cupid hadn't considered the possibility that his brothers would go to such an extreme to protect Ellie as to form an alliance with their most formidable enemies outside of the Titan Pit. Phorcys, otherwise known as the Old Man in the Sea, and his mermaid, Keto, were the parents of the monsters. Scylla, Charybdis, Echidna, and Chimera were loyal to their parents, unlike Ladon who served Hera in the garden of the Hesperides and Cerberus and the Hydra who served Hades. If Phorcys and Keto had agreed to protect the twins and Ellie, Cupid's plan of saving his brothers was pointless.

"Only one of the twins will have gone to Phorcys's castle at the bottom of the sea," Athena pointed out. "The other would have to remain behind to protect the mortal, on an island perhaps."

"Hecate needs more time to perform her location spell," Demeter said. "She's working as fast and as hard as she can."

"Meanwhile, we should split up," Ares said. "While some of us confront Phorcys, the others should search every island on the Ionian Sea."

After hours of lying in the hollowed-out tree talking with Phobos and Deimos about everything from favorite famous athletes to favorite Netflix shows to future aspirations—Ellie confided in them that she hoped to go professional with softball after she graduates—Ellie must have fallen asleep, because suddenly she was awakened by a distant scream.

Ellie sat up. "What was that?"

Night must have fallen, too, because not a single ray from the sun god had broken through the canopy, and although light radiated from the gods on either side of her, outside of the hollowed-out tree, it was nothing but darkness.

"Circe," Deimos said. "Maybe Zeus is torturing her because he thinks she knows where we are."

Phobos shook his head. "I think she's just crazy."

Suddenly a beautiful face with bright glowing eyes surrounded by braids of bright yellow hair poked through the entrance of the hollowed-out tree. "What are you doing in my bed?"

"*Your* bed?" Deimos climbed to his feet. "Don't you sleep in your *house*?"

Ellie realized the face belonged to Circe.

"Never at night," the witch replied. "Because of the blood that pours from my walls. I bet you wouldn't be able to sleep through it, either. It's horrifying. On the other hand, look who I'm talking to: Phobos and Deimos."

Ellie glanced nervously at each of the twins.

"Now, why are you here?" Circe demanded. "And are you friends or foes?"

"Friends," Phobos said.

"We thought Hecate made this bed for us," Deimos said.

"She told us to meet her here," Ellie added.

"And who are you?" Circe moved closer to Ellie and sniffed her.

"Um…" Ellie wasn't sure what to say.

"A mortal? She looks delicious."

Phobos climbed to his feet and helped Ellie to hers. "We'll get out of your hair."

"Nonsense," Circe said. "There's no reason for you to leave. Lie back down and make room for me, and maybe I'll get to sleep for once, so long as Fear and Panic keep their powers to themselves."

Ellie gave each twin another nervous glance. Were they really going to share a bed with a crazy powerful witch?

"We don't want to impose," Phobos said.

"Thanks, anyway," Deimos said.

"If you were an imposition, I'd turn you out. As it is, you're on the verge of offending me. Now sleep!" Circe threw handfuls of pollen at them.

Ellie stumbled to her knees. Phobos and Deimos fell back on the bed beside her. Ellie's face hit one of the pillows, and then everything went dark.

Cupid wished he'd gone with his father and Zeus and the others to Phorcys and Keto's castle at the bottom of the ocean instead of traipsing around every island with his mother, Poseidon, and Rhode. For one, Poseidon was a grump. Two, Poseidon and Rhode bickered the entire time. And three, Aphrodite refused to speak with Cupid because she was still angry with him for saving Ellie.

Cupid would much rather battle the most vicious monsters of the seven seas than be in the company of these three.

But Ares had wanted Cupid and Aphrodite to stay with Poseidon, to make sure he didn't kill Ellie or mistreat whichever twin might be guarding her.

So, Cupid suffered in silence as he flew behind the others. Taking the lead was Poseidon, carrying his trident in one hand and his golden net, draped over his shoulder, in the other. They hopped from one island to the next, beginning with the seven biggest islands, where they split up to search every house in every village and every ship in every harbor. When they found no sign of the fugitives on the big islands, they flew to the small, uninhabited ones and searched through caves and brush. They even went to Cyclopes Island and enlisted the help of Poseidon's son, the cyclops Polyphemus, but they found no trace of Cupid's brothers or the mortal there, either.

"The only place we haven't looked is Circe's Island," Poseidon said.

"They wouldn't go there, Father," Rhode objected. "Let's not waste any more of our time."

"That's precisely why they *would* hide there," Poseidon said. "Because they think it's the last place anyone would look for them."

Cupid finally spoke up. "I agree with Rhode. My brothers are terrified of Circe. Deimos still has a scar she gave him centuries ago. They've never set foot on that island since."

"Poseidon has a point," Aphrodite said. "To Circe's Island it is."

"Then we better hurry," Rhode said, following her father, who, once again, took the lead. "Helios will be coming back around soon, and I don't want him to know what I'm up to. He'll say I was meddling where I shouldn't have, but I care about Mount Olympus, even if he doesn't."

Poseidon told Rhode to quit yammering, or she'd give them away. In silence, they flew beneath the canopy of twisted trees trying not to gag on the toxic fumes.

As Cupid scrutinized the bushes and trees of Circe's freaky forest, he could sense his brothers' contentment. He couldn't sense their location, but he could tell that, wherever they were, they were happy. A pang of guilt penetrated his heart as he continued the search. The only way to help his brothers was to cure them, even if it meant he had to hurt them first.

"Got you!" Poseidon called out as he threw his net into a hollowed-out tree.

"We got all three of them!" Rhode cried.

"No thanks to you," Poseidon chided. "If we'd taken *your* advice, we would have missed them."

"It's *all* thanks to me, Father! You forget who went behind her husband's back to lead you to this sea!"

Cupid ignored the bickering, just as he ignored the telepathic prayers of desperation from his brothers, trapped beneath the net with Ellie, gaping and speechless, between them.

"Let's get them to Mount Olympus immediately," Aphrodite said. "I don't want my sons to suffer any more than is necessary."

Ellie awoke with a start and found herself flying in a chariot in the early morning dawn. Beside her was a stranger with long black and white hair fanning in the wind from beneath the helm of invisibility.

"Who are you?" Ellie asked. "And where are Phobos and Deimos?"

"My name is Hecate," the driver said. "Lord Hades sent me to rescue you. I couldn't get to Phobos and Deimos in time. Poseidon and his search party found you just as I did."

"What?" Ellie was scared and confused.

"It's a miracle I got you out when I did," Hecate said. "If Circe hadn't been there to act as my decoy, I don't think I'd have managed it."

"I don't understand. Circe was helping us?"

"Not intentionally, no." Hecate tugged on the reins, and the chariot made a sharp right, nearly knocking Ellie into the goddess seated beside her. "And, unfortunately, the spell I cast on her won't last long."

"Where are we going?" Ellie asked.

"To the Underworld."

Cupid stood in the great hall of Mount Olympus guarding his brothers and Ellie, who huddled together beneath Poseidon's golden net in the middle of the room. Rhode hadn't accompanied them to Mount Olympus, because she had an appointment with her husband. And, when Cupid, his mother, and Poseidon had arrived with their prisoners, Hermes had appeared moments after, begging for help with a battle against Phorcys.

Although Cupid didn't know the details, he imagined that the bull-headed Zeus raged into the Old Man of the Sea's castle, spitting accusations. And Cupid imagined that Phorcys took offense, since, in the end, Phobos and Deimos *hadn't* gone to him with the hope of forming an alliance. They'd been hiding with Ellie in Circe's forest all this time.

But why? Why would his brothers hide there when they must have known they'd be found eventually? Had they gone to Circe for help?

Cupid and his prisoners hadn't been alone in the great hall long when Deimos said, "Please, Cupid. Don't do this. Set us free. I beg you."

"It's for your own good that I keep you in that net," Cupid said, his heart aching for them.

"Let Ellie go," Phobos said. "You know what the others will do to her."

"What will they do to her?" Ellie asked Phobos.

"To you," Phobos said gently.

"Why me? What have I done but given you a simple sleeping spell?"

Phobos grabbed her shoulders. "Circe? Where's Ellie?"

"How should I know?"

Cupid punched his fist into his hand. How had the mortal gotten away?

"Who did this to you?" Cupid asked. "Or are you working with someone?"

The witch shrugged. "I had no idea I'd been transformed until just now. I rather enjoyed how protective you boys have been of me. Now I understand why."

Deimos and Phobos each took a step back from the witch.

Deimos turned to Cupid. "You have no idea where Ellie is?"

"No," Cupid said. "Someone must have helped her. Do either of you know who?"

Phobos and Deimos shook their heads, though Cupid wasn't convinced that they didn't know more.

Then he realized he didn't need Ellie. His plan could still work, as long as his brothers were looking at Ellie's image when he shot them with the arrows of hate. But Cupid had no idea how long Circe would remain in Ellie's image. He needed to act fast to get the council back to Mount Olympus, so the powers of the twins could be stripped and the arrows shot before Circe returned to her natural form.

Cupid clasped his hands together. "Don't tell the others it's Circe, or they'll keep searching for Ellie until they kill her."

"How do we keep Circe from telling them the truth?" Deimos asked.

"Or Apollo from recognizing a falsehood?" Phobos asked.

"If the witch doesn't speak, we might get away with it," Cupid said. "We'll have to act fast, before the gods attempt to question her."

"Just let us go," Deimos begged.

"Let us enjoy the gift you've given us for as long as we can," Phobos said.

"Trust me, brothers," Cupid said. "I'm doing the right thing by you."

"If you carry out your plan, I'll never forgive you," Phobos said.

"And neither will I," Deimos added.

"You say that now, but you'll thank me later." Cupid turned to Circe. "There's got to be something you want that I can use to buy your silence."

"I want love," she said. "I've been alone for ages and ages. I want someone to love me like these boys love the mortal."

Cupid couldn't imagine saddling anyone—mortal or god—with this crazy witch, but he felt he had no choice.

"You have my word," Cupid said. "You stay silent, and when this is all over, I'll find you a match."

"Swear on the River Styx," Circe demanded.

Cupid sighed. "I swear on the River Styx that I'll find you a match if you cooperate with me."

The witch spit on the floor—Cupid supposed it was to seal their deal—then Cupid summoned Pegasus to keep watch over the prisoners while he rushed to retrieve the others from the Ionian Sea.

<u>CHAPTER NINETEEN</u>

The Underworld and a Battle at Sea

Ellie clung to the side of the golden chariot as the two black horses dragged it across the dark sky. They were moving much faster than Selene's chariot or Helios's golden cup.

Hecate glanced over at her. "We're almost there. Hang on."

Suddenly, the two horses stopped and dived toward the ground at a frightening speed, faster than any roller coaster Ellie had ever ridden.

"Are we gonna crash?" Ellie asked, her knuckles white.

"No, but it's about to get intense. Don't scream. We can't afford to draw attention to ourselves."

Ellie clenched her jaw and held on tighter. *Please don't let me die.*

The chariot flew through a deep crevice in the ground, and then turned sharply to the left, nearly tossing Ellie out of it. They took another sharp turn to the right before they emerged into an enormous cavern.

They slowed before a tall iron gate—as tall as a three-story building. Standing in front of it was a black creature who was nearly as tall. Ellie covered her mouth when she realized the creature had three ferocious dog heads, like Fluffy in the *Harry Potter* series.

"This must be a major drug trip," Ellie whispered to herself.

Down below, where two rivers met, an old man was pulling a raft toward the gate. He had three passengers aboard. One was a beautiful teenaged boy. The other two were hard to make out, because they were transparent, like ghosts.

The chariot flew over and past the raft, through the gate, and along a river of fire before entering a stone building with a floor covered in hay.

Hecate brought the chariot to a halt. "I'll just unbridle Swift and Sure, and then we'll be on our way. Wait in the chariot."

"On our way where?" Ellie asked.

"Just wait in the chariot."

Ellie closed her eyes and tried to pray to Phobos and Deimos. *Phobos and Deimos, I don't know if you can hear me, but someone, a goddess, I think, named Hecate brought me to a really strange place underground. There was a tall gate with a creature like Fluffy from Harry Potter, and there are rivers—one made of fire. Where the hell am I and can you please come and get me?*

Ellie tried not to cry when the goddess appeared at her side with the helm in her hand and said, "Follow me."

When Cupid reached the outskirts of Phorcys and Keto's castle, he was dismayed by what he saw. Echidna had Ares trapped in a coil of her serpent's tail and was whipping the end of the tail at Athena. Athena, maneuvering in the sea to avoid the attacks, held her spear at the ready as she waited for the right moment to counter.

Phorcys and Keto hung, suspended and paralyzed in the water, probably from Poseidon's trident. Persephone and Aphrodite bound them in ropes, since one never knew how long paralysis from the trident would last. Chimera was floundering opposite them with Hephaestus's legs hanging from her lion's mouth and Hermes holding onto him. Chimera appeared to be trying to swallow Hephaestus instead of biting him in half. As all the gods knew, being swallowed was the worst fate to befall an immortal because it was a very difficult trap to escape. Athena's mother, Metis, was still trapped in Zeus's belly and had been for centuries.

Zeus and Hera were fighting off Scylla's six long necks and grisly heads, along with her two giant pincers and eight tentacles, while Artemis and Apollo shot arrows into the gaping mouth of Charybdis.

Cupid realized the reason they hadn't god-traveled out of there was that they couldn't risk Hephaestus getting swallowed.

Poseidon, who hovered with his trident opposite Echidna, shouted to him, "Help Athena free Ares! I can't strike her until you do!"

Cupid considered shooting Echidna in the heart as she gazed on her prisoner, but he couldn't risk her running off with him. So, instead, he conjured his sword and swung at the thick tail hurling through the water.

His presence caused Echidna to change directions, which Athena wisely anticipated. Athena drove her spear into Echidna's heart and her thick tail uncoiled.

As soon as Cupid had pulled his father free, Poseidon shot Echidna with his trident and paralyzed her. Cupid and Ares bound her with rope, while Athena retrieved her spear from the monster's heart.

Cupid, Ares, and Athena then focused their efforts on Chimera until Hephaestus was free, and, at last, the exhausted Olympians could retreat to the great hall, where their prisoners were waiting.

Ellie followed the black-and-white haired goddess known as Hecate from the chariot along the river of fire. It flowed through a cavernous and winding tunnel. She glanced back, wondering if she should make a run for it, but she had no idea where she was or where she would run to.

Soon the tunnel opened into a large—and beautiful—cavern. The light from the fire reflected off the stone walls, stalagmites, and stalactites. Ellie noticed little round emeralds, rubies, and diamonds embedded in places in the stone walls, and these, too, sparkled. It seemed as if the goddess had led Ellie into another dimension—a fairy dimension.

In the center of this very large cavern was what appeared to be a castle or palace of sorts. Hecate led them to a tall wooden door and knocked.

"Enter!" a deep voice called from inside the palace.

Hecate opened the door and crossed the threshold. Ellie hesitated, frightened of what might be waiting on the other side.

The goddess beckoned Ellie to follow with a wave of her hand. "Let's not keep the lord waiting."

Ellie swallowed hard, attempting to wet her now very dry throat, as she followed Hecate into what appeared to be a throne room, because across from them, sitting on a golden high-back chair, was a beautiful god wearing a crown on his curly black head.

After Hecate had given the helm to the god, he secured it in a chest below his seat. Then he sat back down, crossed one leg over the other, and said, "So, this is the girl that's caused all the commotion among the Olympians?"

"Yes, Lord Hades," Hecate replied. "This is Ellie Beaufort." Hecate turned to Ellie. "I'd like you to meet Lord Hades, God of the Underworld."

Ellie didn't know whether she was expected to curtsy, kneel, or bow, so she did a combination in a kind of genuflection she'd seen the Catholics do when she went with her teammate Maria to mass before their first big game.

"I'm sure you're wondering why we brought you here," the god said.

Ellie wondered if she was doing that thing again, where she accidentally prayed her thoughts, because it was like he was reading her mind.

"Yes, but I'm also wondering where Phobos and Deimos are. Do you know what's happened to them?"

"They've been taken to Mount Olympus," Lord Hades said. "Cupid plans to convince the council to support Zeus in taking away Phobos and Deimos's godly powers. Cupid then plans to shoot his brothers with arrows of hate, to neutralize their feelings of love and desire for you."

"Can he do that?" Ellie asked. In her mind, she thought, *Please say no, please say no, please say no.*

"Yes," Hades replied.

"But only if the twins are gazing upon you or an image of you," Hecate added.

Ellie's heart leapt. "Is that why I'm here? You're helping me?"

"Yes and no," the god said.

Ellie frowned.

"What the others do with Phobos and Deimos is of no concern to me," Hades said.

"But Cupid can't do it without me, right?" Ellie asked.

"He can with your image," Hecate said. "A photo of you, or, say, perhaps a witch who has been spelled to look like you."

Ellie's stomach dropped, as if she were falling through the sky again. "Is that what you did to Circe?"

Hecate nodded. "But it won't last more than a day. They'll have to work fast if they want to use her as your image."

Ellie hoped and prayed that Cupid's plan would fail. She couldn't imagine how brokenhearted she'd be if the twins no longer loved her.

"We didn't bring you to help you with Phobos and Deimos," Hades said. "We brought you here to spare ourselves from the reckoning."

"D-does that mean you're going to kill me?" Ellie asked as her knees quaked.

Hades picked at his curly black beard. "In a way, yes."

Once the battle-tired Olympians had taken their seats on their thrones along the perimeter of the great hall, Cupid asked if he could address the court.

"Go ahead," Zeus said.

Cupid told the entire council what he had done to protect Ellie Beaufort. He explained that he had not been informed of the prophecy and wanted to spare an innocent girl by hiding her away until his mother had moved on. He told about Phobos and Deimos and the arrows, and he confessed his sincere regret for burdening his brothers by binding their hearts to a mortal. He begged the court to support Zeus in stripping his brothers' powers so that arrows of hate could be used to neutralize the arrows of love. Then, the court could decide what to do with Ellie Beaufort, but he hoped he could end his brothers' misery before any action was taken against the mortal.

Cupid could see that the gods were moved by his story and that they wanted to spare his brothers. This impression was solidified when Zeus called for a vote, and all were in favor of stripping the twins of their power—all save Psyche, but only the majority of the Olympians were needed.

"Wait!" Phobos cried after the vote had been cast. "Don't I and my brother have the right to speak for ourselves?"

"Please, Lord Zeus," Deimos said. "Please fellow Olympians. Hear what we have to say."

Cupid told his brothers telepathically that they were only further endangering Ellie Beaufort's life by stalling. Circe could return to her natural form at any moment, and the other gods would care more about hunting Ellie down than about sparing Phobos and Deimos from an eternity of agony.

But they didn't heed his warning.

"Speak, Phobos," Zeus said. "Then we will hear from your brother."

Phobos glanced back at Cupid before turning to face Zeus. "I would rather have a short but true and deep love than no love at all. Cupid says he'll match me with an immortal after this ordeal, but you and I know that's not going to happen. My parents don't want their children to find love. We all know what Cupid had to go through to get Psyche. And even though Harmonia was permitted to marry, it was to a mortal king, and it was allowed so the two of them could create an army of demigods for my father."

"Phobos!" Ares jumped to his feet. "How dare you?"

"Do you deny it?" Deimos asked. "Phobos and I have been made to serve all of you because you need the mortals to fear you, and you need them to panic at the thought of a world without gods. But each of you have had loves, and some of you still do."

"Deimos and I just want this one love for her natural life," Phobos said. "We swear not to shirk our duties."

"You can't *both* have her," Hera said.

"Each of you risks breaking the heart of your brother," Artemis added.

"Let us worry about that," Phobos said.

"Just give us the chance at love," Deimos said. "Hera, you of all the gods must understand. Your love for Zeus is unfailing."

"What about the prophecy?" Apollo asked.

"Exactly," Hermes said.

Athena stepped forward. "Have you not heard of the girl's connection with the fate of Mount Olympus?"

The other gods murmured until Zeus silenced them and asked Phobos and Deimos if they had anything to say about the prophecy.

"If the Fates have deemed it, there's nothing you can do," Deimos said.

The gods argued among themselves so that Zeus had to silence them again.

Cupid stepped forward. "These speeches from my brothers can't be trusted. They're under the influence of the arrows and will say anything to fulfill their desire for Ellie Beaufort. You've already agreed to strip them of their powers. I beg that we move forward and decide what to do about the mortal afterward, without my brothers' interference."

"Hear, hear!" Aphrodite cried.

CHAPTER TWENTY

Remedies

Ellie looked up at the lord of the underworld with wide eyes. "You *are* going to kill me?"

"Not for the reason you think," Hades said, which clarified nothing for Ellie.

Ellie glanced at Hecate, hoping for some clue as to whether these gods were her friends or her foes, but Hecate only waited patiently for Hades to continue.

With one leg crossed over the other, the lord of the Underworld sat back on his throne and picked his beard. "You see, Ellie, the Fates have revealed that you are connected with a day of reckoning for the Olympians."

Ellie clasped her hands behind her back to control her trembling. It wasn't exactly fear that had overwhelmed her. It was anxiety. "I don't know what that means."

"None of us knows for certain," Hades said. "Prophecies tend to be fuzzy. The Fates warn us that it's best not to know what the future holds, and yet we can't resist trying to predict it. With prophets like Apollo and my good friend Hecate seeing bits and pieces of what's to come, we can't help but respond when those visions reveal the fall of Mount Olympus."

"What has that got to do with me?" Ellie asked with trembling lips.

"What do you know about the Olympians, Ellie?" Hades asked.

"Very little," she admitted. "I didn't know you existed until Cupid and Psyche kidnapped me—or rescued me."

"There was a time when *mortals* didn't exist. Did you know that?"

Ellie shook her head.

"My brother Zeus…" Hades paused. "Isn't sibling love complicated?"

For once, Ellie could relate to what the god was saying. "Yes. It is."

"You see, my father cared more for himself than his children. I know this because when he heard a prophecy that one of his sons would one day take his place, instead of being pleased to pass on his legacy to that son, he decided to swallow his children, one by one, as soon as they were born. Have you heard that story?"

Ellie shook her head.

"When the sixth child was born, my mother had finally decided she'd had enough—though it was too bad it took sacrificing five of her children for her to arrive at that point. Anyway, she gave my father a rock wrapped in a blanket to swallow and hid my brother Zeus. When he became of age, Zeus rescued the rest of us from our father's belly, and we helped him to trap our father in the Titan Pit. We were indebted to Zeus, still feel indebted to him. You can understand that, can't you, Ellie?"

Ellie nodded.

Hades picked at his beard and uncrossed his legs. "It was Zeus's idea to create a race of mortals. It was a good idea. I still believe that today. We gods were already powerful, but we soon discovered that when we were worshipped by mortals, our powers increased."

Hades stood from his chair and stepped down from his throne. Only a few meters away from Ellie, the god began to pace. "But we also had a responsibility now that we'd never had before. My two brothers and I decided to split up the responsibilities between us: Zeus ruled the skies, Poseidon the seas, and I the Underworld, the realm of the dead."

Ellie finally understood where she was. Hecate had said they were going to the Underworld. Hades had just called it the realm of the dead. "Am I dead?"

"Not yet," Hades said. "May I continue?"

Ellie's cheeks burned as she nodded and reminded herself to shut up.

"Some gods took their responsibilities more seriously than others," Hades said. "Some gods were hot and cold—very compassionate and serving of humankind at times and very selfish, indifferent, distracted, or outright cruel at others."

Ellie wondered why the lord of the Underworld was bothering to give her this speech. What did she have to do with any of it?

"I'm getting to that part, Ellie," Hades said, as though he'd heard her.

She realized she'd done that thing again where she'd turned a thought into a prayer.

"Tell me something, Ellie," Hades said. "Do you think life is fair?"

She wondered if it was a trick question.

"It's not a trick. I want your honest answer. Is life fair?"

"No," she said, thinking about her childhood, growing up in the projects with a mom who whored herself to provide food for her and her sister.

"I agree," Hades said. "And even though the gods don't like to admit it, they're at least partly responsible for the stark inequities faced by humankind."

Ellie wondered what Phobos and Deimos would say about that.

"What I'm driving at, Ellie, is that, although life isn't fair, *death* is. I am a *just* ruler. I am a *fair* ruler. When people die, they are judged by three impartial kings and then sentenced for their just desserts. The relatively good people—and they don't have to be perfect—go to the Fields of Elysium. The truly bad people go to Tartarus, where the Furies punish each soul according to its failings. And those who are victimized or traumatized to the degree that they can't be held accountable for their actions, those souls go to Erebus to be healed before moving on to the Elysian Fields. That sounds fair, doesn't it?"

Ellie nodded.

"I have a bad reputation among mortals that I find wholly undeserved," Hades said. "But as a just and fair god, I can say that the Olympians deserve a day of reckoning. And I believe that if the gods are performing their duties to the best of their abilities, then they have nothing to fear from this reckoning."

Ellie still didn't understand what this had to do with her or why this god was telling her this.

"I think the Fates sent you as a test, Ellie," Hades said.

"Me? Why me?"

"You're beautiful, talented, and vulnerable," he said. "And you're easy to exploit, easy to kill."

Ellie worried her knees would buckle. *Oh, my god, I'm going to fall on my face.* Suddenly a chair appeared behind her.

"Forgive me," Hades said. "Sit, please."

Ellie, still trembling, sat.

"The Fates, I believe, gave Apollo a vision associating you with the fall of Mount Olympus to see how we would react. Would we kill you— an innocent mortal with so much life still ahead of you? Or would we protect you at our own peril, since we created you and are responsible for you?"

Ellie finally understood what the god was saying, but she still couldn't tell whether Hades meant to kill or protect her. "S-so what are you going to do to me?"

Cupid watched in agony as his brothers were stripped of their godly powers. It didn't look *physically* painful, but Cupid imagined it must be emotionally and psychologically traumatic. Although Phobos and Deimos were still immortal when the ordeal was over, they were as defenseless as men against the other gods. Because of this, it was important to restore their powers as quickly as possible. As loyal as Cupid was to his parents and to Zeus, he'd lived long enough to know that gods couldn't always be trusted not to have agendas of their own. He would never forgive himself if his brothers were swallowed or were put into some other trap from which they could never be freed.

The other gods dimmed themselves, like they did in the presence of mortals, so as not to blind the twins. Cupid was unnerved by his brothers' lack of radiance. Their skin was dull, like a man's.

"I'll never forgive you," Phobos spit from his cage. "Any of you!"

Tears filled Deimos's eyes. "You can still decide to spare us, Cupid. It's not too late."

Cupid fit an arrow of hate to his bow. "Look at Ellie, and this will soon be over."

Psyche beseeched him in prayer to change his mind.

The brothers closed their eyes and refused to open them.

Ares crossed the room, stuck his fingers through the netting, and held Phobos's face toward Circe, while swift Hermes opened one of Phobos's eyelids. Phobos grunted and struggled as hard as any man could, but the other gods easily overpowered him.

Cupid shot the arrow of hate into Phobos's heart.

Deimos fell to his knees and cried. "Please don't! I beg you, Cupid! If you have any love for me, you won't do this!"

Ares moved to his other son, stuck his fingers through the net, and grabbed Deimos's face, pointing it toward Circe. Then Hermes lifted the lid of Deimos's left eye. Deimos shouted his pleas, but Cupid didn't let them dissuade him from his purpose. He fit the second arrow of hate to his bow and shot Deimos in the heart.

"I'm giving you a choice," Hades said to Ellie. "You can remain as you are, vulnerable to the attacks of the other gods—and make no mistake, they will come for you. Or I can make you a goddess, an immortal, like me."

"Huh?" Ellie wasn't sure she'd heard him correctly.

"There's a catch. There always is. Nothing in life is free."

Ellie stared back at Hades, gaping. Was he serious about making her like him? If so, that would mean she could be with one of the twins forever. She could spare one of them from an eternity of misery—though she had no idea which she would choose.

And what about her dreams of becoming a professional softball player? Could she still do that as a goddess? Would she still want to? Maybe as a goddess, she could give her mother and sister all the things they always wanted and never were able to have.

"What's the catch?" she finally asked.

"It's going to hurt like hell," he said. "Because I'll have to kill you first."

Cupid wiped his tears with the back of his hand as he watched his brothers slump to the floor. Phobos lay on his side, curled up like a fetus. Deimos sat back on his knees and covered his face. Cupid wondered how long it would take them to realize he'd just set them free.

Cupid turned to Zeus. "Can you reinstate their powers now, lord Zeus? The deed is done."

"We better kill the mortal first," Poseidon said. "Just in case Phobos and Deimos have residual feelings for her."

"Agreed," Zeus said. "Remove your net and bring her to me."

Poseidon lifted his net from the prisoners, and grabbed Circe's arm, believing it to belong to the mortal, Ellie Beaufort.

Cupid wasn't sure how he was going to get out of this mess. If the others discovered that it was Circe, and not the mortal, Cupid's goose was cooked. There was no way the witch was going to remain silent as the gods tried to kill her.

In a moment of clarity, Cupid said, "I feel responsible, Lord Zeus. I should be the one to remedy our problem."

Without waiting for anyone to object, Cupid approached the witch from behind, conjured his sword, and sliced her head from her body.

"Cupid, no!" Psyche wailed.

There was a gasp among the gods. They had probably envisioned a death less graphic.

Telepathically, Cupid said to the witch, as her body fell into his arms and her blood spilled down his legs, *I'm sorry, Circe. I promise to preserve your body as it waits for your soul's return. And I'll keep my oath about your match.*

Cupid carried the limp body of the witch, still in Ellie's form, and laid her at the feet of Zeus. Then he placed her head against her neck.

When Thanatos arrived to take Circe's soul, he gave Cupid a bewildered look but said nothing. Cupid decided then and there that he would someday do something nice for Death, even though he and his duties were repugnant to him.

But Thanatos's silence was for naught, because the moment the soul left its body, the body reverted to its natural form.

CHAPTER TWENTY-ONE

Proposals

Ellie sat in Hades's throne room thinking over what she'd been told. The lord of the Underworld had just explained that apotheosis—the transformation of a mortal into an immortal being—required the sanction of the most powerful god among them: Zeus. Hades had said that Zeus would never agree to change Ellie into a goddess, because it would be easier for him to kill her, and because there was no guarantee that making her immortal would change the prophecy or satisfy the reckoning.

But, according to Hades, Hecate knew of another way.

Hecate had then explained that she would anoint Ellie from head to toe with ambrosia from Mount Olympus. Then, Ellie would be placed in the hearth, where her mortal body would burn so her immortal body could be reborn.

Ellie was having a difficult time digesting that last part: her body would have to burn in order to be reborn as a goddess.

"I'm sure you have questions," Hades said as he sat back down on his throne.

"Can you put me under, with drugs or something?" Ellie asked. "So I don't feel it?"

Hecate shook her head. "Unfortunately, for the soul to be reborn as an immortal, it must be aware, conscious of the death, or the transformation won't succeed."

"Has this process ever failed before?" Ellie asked. "Is there a chance I could die, anyway?"

"It's only ever been attempted twice, that I know of," Hecate said. "And it worked both times."

"And there's something else you should know," Hades said. "The transformation will reverse itself in three months, if you don't declare your purpose as a member of our pantheon."

"What does that mean?" Ellie asked.

"It means two things," Hecate said. "First, you have a choice. If you don't want to remain an immortal, simply fail to declare yourself, and, in three months, your immortality will vanish. And second, if you decide you *do* want to remain a goddess, you'll need to serve a purpose for humanity or the world in some way."

"I'll need to what?"

"Serve," Hades said.

"For example, I serve two purposes," Hecate explained. "As the goddess of the crossroads, I help mortals make the most difficult decisions of their lives. As the goddess of witchcraft, I lead the mortal covens of the world. You only need one, though, for the transformation to stick."

"A problem to consider," Hades said, "is that we have many, many gods already serving in almost every capacity you can think of. It might be difficult to find an area that is underserviced."

"Your purpose must be unique," Hecate clarified. "You can't choose to serve in a way that another deity already fulfills."

"But aren't Aphrodite and Cupid both gods of love?" Ellie asked. "And don't Psyche and Hera work together to save marriages?"

Hades crossed one leg over the other and scratched his black, curly beard. "Good questions, but the answer is no. Aphrodite is the goddess of love and beauty. She looks for opportunities to bring fated lovers together and to help them to see the beauty in one another. But she often enjoys bringing lovers together who aren't fated, purely for her own entertainment. Whereas Eros—the god you call Cupid—he has more to do with desire—with that deep, urgent need to always be with the one you love. His arrows bond lovers for life, so he is less casual than his mother with the people he unites. They do often work together, but they are doing different things."

"And what about Hera and Psyche?" Ellie asked.

"Hera is the goddess of marriage and families," Hades explained. "She focuses more on keeping the family unit together, and she also oversees pregnancy and childbirth. Psyche is the goddess of sacred un- ions. After her husband bonds lovers for life, Psyche works to help them through the ups and downs that all people go through, even when they are deeply in love."

Ellie understood the differences now. She supposed that if she did choose to become a goddess, she would need a list of what jobs were already taken, so she could figure out her unique purpose. "Is there a list of all the gods and what they do?"

Hades chuckled. "Indeed, I believe there is. It's on something called the Internet."

Hecate joined the lord of the Underworld in a laugh, but Ellie was too frightened and overwhelmed to laugh with them.

"One more question," Ellie said.

"Ask as many as you'd like," Hades said, "but please be aware that we don't have an infinite amount of time. I cannot predict when the others will realize that you're missing, nor can I guess when they'll figure out that you're with me."

"Okay." Ellie's teeth chattered. The pressure was on, and her anxiety was severe. "If I choose to return to my normal life, will I have to burn again?"

"No," Hecate replied. "Your soul will simply revert. I don't think you feel much of anything at all."

"And what if I declare my purpose in three months but later change my mind. Could I still go back to my normal life?"

"Not without going mad," Hades said. "If gods abandon their duties, they gradually go insane."

Ellie shuddered. "Would I be able to visit my family as a goddess?"

"As often as you like," Hecate said.

"Can I give them anything I want—like a mansion, fancy cars, fine jewelry?"

"Indeed, you can," Hades said. "But there's one more thing I think you need to understand. Becoming a goddess won't make you invincible. Although it's true that you cannot permanently die…"

"What do you mean by 'permanently'?"

Hades picked at his beard. "If another god were to slice off your head, it would kill you. Your soul would be taken by Thanatos to Tartarus. But once your immortal body healed, it would call your soul back to it."

"Oh."

"So, you see, you can still suffer death many times," Hades said. "And death isn't the worst ordeal for a god."

"It's not?"

"If a god swears an oath on the River Styx," Hecate began, "and later breaks it, the Maenads will rip that god apart, limb by limb, once a year."

Ellie didn't want to ask what the Maenads were. She'd just be sure never to swear on the River Styx.

"The very worst—and I'm speaking from experience," Hades began, "is to be swallowed by another god. There's nothing worse than that."

Ellie pulled on her fingers and bit her lips as she digested the information and considered their proposal. She had no idea how she would serve, but she'd have three months to figure it out. As a goddess, she could give her family and friends everything they ever wanted. She could also help people who couldn't help themselves, like other kids growing up in the projects, kids who don't always know where their next meal is coming from. Ellie could do all the things that she saw Phobos and

Deimos and Cupid and Psyche do. Maybe she could even live in a castle as wonderful as theirs.

Most of all, she could share her eternity with Phobos or Deimos—she didn't know which, but an immortal life would give her plenty of time to choose.

One thing nagging at the back of Ellie's mind was the question of motives. If Hades really believed that saving her was the answer to sparing Mount Olympus from the reckoning, why hadn't he pitched his argument to the other gods? He might have convinced Zeus to transform her and, in so doing, would have spared her the unimaginable pain of burning alive.

Is there something else you're after, lord of the Underworld? she wondered.

Hades waved a finger at her. "You're smarter than you look."

That didn't sound like a compliment to Ellie.

"Although I doubt that I could have convinced Zeus and the other Olympians that saving you was the answer," Hades began, "I didn't invest my time in trying because I want to be the one to save Mount Olympus. For reasons we won't get into, the Olympians despise me. I want them to feel beholden to me."

If Hades was willing to bet his reputation on Ellie's transformation, he must truly believe in what he was proposing.

Was there anything else she hadn't thought of? Could this be some kind of trick that she couldn't see coming?

Ellie decided that the opportunity to spend an eternity with the person she loved—whether it was Phobos or Deimos—was worth taking a chance on Hades and Hecate.

"I'll do it," Ellie said.

Cupid looked from the dead body of Circe to the enraged face of Zeus, trying to hide his trepidation.

"I didn't know," Cupid said, grasping at straws.

He quickly prayed to Apollo and confessed everything to him. *I wanted to spare my brothers an eternity of misery. I wasn't trying to save Ellie Beaufort. Someone tricked me into believing Circe was Ellie. I only discovered the truth after we'd brought her here, and Ellie was nowhere to be found. Keep my secret, Apollo, and I promise to cooperate with you whenever you need requited love and desire.*

He glanced at the god of truth and was relieved when he said nothing.

Cupid also prayed to his brothers not to sell him out, reminding them that he was doing all of this to right the wrong he had committed against them.

Surprised by their silence, Cupid glanced back at his brothers. They were still covering their faces and weeping. Had the arrows of hate not worked on them?

Of course, they had, he thought. There was no reason they shouldn't have.

He caught his mother looking at him in horror. She didn't have to pray to him for Cupid to know what she was thinking. She believed he meant to undermine her and the other Olympians. She believed he'd used Circe to trick them and to save Ellie.

Mother, he prayed. *I want Ellie Beaufort dead just as much as the rest of you.*

Her expression told him she wasn't convinced. Again, no words were needed.

As he turned back to face Zeus, he also caught a glimpse of his father glaring at him with suspicion. He prayed the same thing to his father as he had to his mother, but again, to no real effect.

Psyche gave him a timid smile and prayed, *I couldn't be prouder. Thank you for protecting the girl.*

He ignored his wife's prayers and turned to Zeus. "I'll make it my mission to find the mortal and kill her myself."

Psyche's urgent prayer interrupted his thoughts. *What are you saying? Is this another trick?*

He ignored her again. "I'll make this right, Lord Zeus, if you'll give me the chance. I promise."

Zeus seemed to consider Cupid's proposal. Then he said, "Eros, son of Ares and Aphrodite, do you swear on the River Styx that you had no knowledge that this imposter was the witch Circe?"

Ellie followed Hecate out of the throne room—not through the door they had entered, but through a hall leading them further into the palace. Ellie was trembling as if the temperature were below freezing, but it wasn't the cold that had her body shaking out of control; it was the anticipation of the heat.

Hecate led her into a small chamber with a hearth that ran the length of the room, which was perhaps ten or twelve feet. At the bottom of the hearth was a bed of ash, and above it was an iron grate. The grate consisted of scrollwork resembling a tree with many branches curling from the center trunk. Ellie realized she would be expected to lie on that grate. She was looking at the very spot where she was to burn.

Hecate closed the door behind them and snapped her fingers. Ellie's clothes and boots were replaced with a simple white smock that opened to the front and was tied at the neckline with a thin ribbon.

"I need to anoint you with the ambrosia," Hecate said. "I apologize in advance if this makes you feel uncomfortable."

"I'm sure this will be the least uncomfortable part," Ellie said nervously.

A golden goblet appeared in each of Hecate's hands. She handed one of the cups to Ellie. "Drink this. It's wine, to help you relax."

Ellie took the cup in her trembling hands but knew nothing short of morphine would relax her. Her hands were shaking so wildly, that she was afraid she'd spill the wine when she attempted to bring the goblet to her lips. And yet, she didn't feel afraid or panicky about what she was going to do. She wondered if this meant that Phobos and Deimos were too far away to affect her.

Instead, it was worry and anxiety that had her trembling uncontrollably. She hoped she was making the right decision, not just for herself, not just for her family, but for Phobos and Deimos. Would they want her to do this? She wished she could ask them.

"Maybe you should do it," Ellie finally said when her jittery hands had made it impossible for her to drink from the heavy goblet.

Hecate took the cup and held it to Ellie's lips. With chattering teeth and quivering lips, Ellie sipped. The wine was smooth, but Ellie was too nervous to notice the taste of it. Hecate tilted the cup, and Ellie drank it up, to the very last drop.

Then the wine goblet vanished, and Hecate said, "Perhaps you should lie down on the grate while I perform the anointing. I think you're too weak to stand."

As Ellie climbed into the hearth and lay on her back on the iron grate, she began to have second thoughts about becoming a goddess—not because she didn't want to become powerful and immortal, but because she worried that the gods might be tricking her into letting them kill her.

"I don't know if I can do it," she said when Hecate began to rub the ambrosia onto Ellie's skin.

"I won't force you," Hecate said as she continued to apply the sticky liquid. "But I can tell you that it will be over very quickly."

"Would you swear on the River Styx that you aren't secretly trying to kill me?" Ellie asked the goddess.

"I swear on the River Styx," Hecate said gently. "I am trying to save your life by making you immortal."

"Promise?" Tears fell from Ellie's eyes, and her teeth chattered more wildly than before.

"I promise."

Ellie closed her eyes and focused on the time she spent with Phobos and Deimos. She thought about how they made her feel when they touched her. She began to imagine that they were with her, touching her now. Ellie could feel their fingers rubbing her arms, her hands, her fingers. Then they rubbed her legs, her knees, her shins, her feet, and her toes. Deimos rubbed one breast as Phobos rubbed the other. She imagined herself on the feather bed in the hollowed-out tree with Phobos on one side of her and Deimos on the other. Phobos's fingers had found the sweet spot, and Deimos's hands massaged her breasts. Deimos's tongue caressed her ear as Phobos bit her neck.

She wasn't sure if the gods could hear her prayers from this far away, but, just in case they could, she decided to pray to them as a mortal one last time.

Silently, she said, *I love you, Phobos*. And then she said, *I love you, Deimos*.

And then the flames burst through the grate and engulfed her.

CHAPTER TWENTY-TWO

The Condemned

Cupid could not swear on the River Styx that he had been unaware of Circe's identity, and when he tried to back-pedal, to explain what had really happened and why he had acted in the manner he had, Zeus interrupted him with vicious accusations of sedition.

With tears stinging his eyes, Cupid glanced first at his mother and then at his father, but they still had no words to give him, nor did they show any sign of support for their son. They appeared heartbroken, disappointed, and deflated, but they did not speak up on Cupid's behalf.

Cupid turned to his beautiful wife, but she couldn't even look at him.

When he glanced back at his brothers, he noticed they had stood up, wearing shock on their faces.

Phobos lifted his palms. "Cupid was tricked. We all were."

"We didn't know it was Circe until moments before you returned," Deimos said.

"Our brother was trying to help us." Phobos briefly met Cupid's gaze. "I understand that now."

"But he wasn't trying to undermine you, Lord Zeus," Deimos said.

Zeus turned to Apollo. "What say you? Why so silent?"

"I sense they speak the truth," Apollo said.

Zeus frowned. "Then you must have known Cupid was lying when he said he didn't know it was Circe."

"I felt sorry for him," Apollo explained.

Zeus's face reddened. He pointed a finger at Cupid. "You lied to me, Eros. You and your brothers played out a lie in front of this sacred court and expected to get away with it. We can't tolerate lies."

"Hear, hear!" Poseidon shouted.

Cupid bowed his head.

"For this you must be punished," Zeus said. "All in agreement, say aye."

The great hall resounded with the voices of the gods in unison.

"All opposed?"

The room was silent. Not a single god spoke on behalf of Cupid.

Zeus lifted his chin. "I hereby sentence you and your brothers to six months of manual labor and servitude, without your powers, at a place of my choosing."

"What?" Phobos cried.

Cupid prayed to him to hold his tongue, saying he'd only make things worse.

"Where will you send them?" Ares asked.

Zeus crossed his arms. "Do you have a suggestion?"

Cupid held his breath as he waited for his father's reply.

"Cupid has a talent with horses," Ares said. "Perhaps you could send him and his brothers to work on a ranch where they can care for the beasts."

"That's an excellent idea, Ares," Zeus acknowledged.

Surprised that his father had helped him, and even more surprised that Zeus had agreed to his father's suggestion, Cupid struggled not to cry tears of relief and gratitude. If he was going to be without his powers, at least he could be in the company of his favorite animal companions.

Artemis stepped forward. "I know of a rancher in Texas who's barely holding on to his operation. He leases some of his land to hunters, to help make ends meet, but he's failing. If these three worked for food and lodging and no wages, it could make a difference for the rancher and his family."

Zeus addressed the court. "All in favor of sending these three without their powers to serve a Texas rancher for six months, say aye."

"Aye," the gods replied.

"All opposed?"

The room was silent.

"It's settled then," Zeus said. "Let us strip Eros of his powers, and then Artemis can do the honors of transporting them to where they shall carry out their sentence."

Cupid glanced across the room at Psyche, who still refused to look at him. Then he felt his powers draining from his body. He began to feel tired and achy. When he looked at his skin, he was disgusted by its lack of radiance. He was without strength, speed, and flight. He was without the ability to hear prayers. Moreover, his beloved bow and arrows had vanished. He was nothing but a miserable man in every way except for his immortality.

"The deed is done," Zeus said. "Artemis may dispatch with the condemned to Texas while the rest of us continue our hunt for the mortal."

"She's already dead," Deimos said, matter-of-factly. "I felt the tether to the arrow of love in my heart go slack."

"I felt it, too," Phobos said.

Athena narrowed her eyes. "Is that possible, Cupid?"

"Yes, it's possible," Aphrodite said. "It happens all the time."

Cupid turned to Athena. "When one partner in a bonded pair passes away, the other partner can feel it. It won't free the remaining partner from deep feelings of love and desire for the one who's gone, but the one left behind will sense that the bond is slack."

Hermes scratched his head. "Didn't the arrows of hate neutralize the bond?"

"They neutralized the feelings," Cupid said. "But not the bond."

"Is it true that you boys no longer feel love and desire for the mortal girl?" Hera asked.

"It's true," Phobos said.

"If I feel anything at all for Ellie Beaufort, it's hate," Deimos said.

Phobos grimaced. "I despise her."

"As much as I would like to say otherwise," Poseidon said, "I don't think we should rely on the boys' *feeling* that the girl is dead."

Hera nodded. "We must discover for ourselves."

"Can't Apollo confirm it?" Artemis asked.

"They believe what they say," Apollo said. "I can't see if what they say is true."

"We can find out easily enough," Persephone said. "Just ask my husband."

"Who would have killed her?" Hephaestus wanted to know.

"Whoever stole her from Circe's island," Phobos said.

As if the sound of her name had called the soul back to its body, the witch's body began to twitch, its head properly connected. Circe's radiance returned to her skin and yellow braids. She opened her luminous eyes and sat up. She seemed momentarily confused before recalling what had happened to her. Then she jumped to her feet and glared at Cupid.

"Tell me, Circe," Zeus began.

The witch turned to glare at the king of the Olympians.

Zeus widened his stance and placed his fists on his hips. "Why did you not reveal your identity when we assumed you were Ellie Beaufort?"

"Cupid promised me love," she said.

A few gasps filled the room. Cupid avoided meeting anyone's eyes.

"Do you know who stole the mortal from your island?" Zeus asked the witch.

"I didn't see her captor," Circe said.

"It was probably Hecate," Phobos said. "She sent us a message to meet her there. It must have been a setup."

"Where is Hecate?" Hermes asked.

"Does anyone know?" Zeus asked. "Demeter? Persephone?"

Both goddesses shook their heads.

"Hermes, go and look for her," Zeus said. "But first go to Hades and get confirmation that Ellie Beaufort is dead."

Hermes vanished.

"Artemis, you can use my chariot to escort the condemned to Texas," Zeus said.

Cupid and his brothers followed the goddess of the hunt down the rainbow steps from the great hall, across the courtyard, and into the garage, where the chariots were parked. Cupid bridled Zeus's horses and bid Pegasus goodbye without explaining why he wouldn't see him for a while.

Sitting in the backseat beside his brothers in the chariot, Cupid asked Phobos and Deimos, "Do you forgive me, then?"

Deimos clenched his jaw and said nothing.

Phobos glared at Cupid. "I understand why you did what you did, but, no, I don't forgive you."

Ellie opened her eyes and gasped for air.

"You need to leave," Hecate said beside her. "Now."

"Huh?" Ellie glanced down at her naked body. It was glowing.

Hecate snapped her fingers, and Ellie was suddenly clothed in a loose lavender blouse, jeans, and flat-heeled boots.

"Hermes is here," Hecate whispered. "I don't have time to take you myself. Do you know how to god-travel?"

Ellie climbed from the grate to her feet. She'd never felt so alive and full of energy. "How to what?"

"If only the helm weren't in the throne room," Hecate muttered.

"What's the problem? I'm a goddess now, right? I mean, look at me!" Ellie was ecstatic. She couldn't wait to show Phobos and Deimos what she'd become. "I can't believe it actually worked!"

"No, you look at me and listen to what I say," Hecate said sharply, but in a low voice. "The other gods need to think you're dead. If they discover what I've done, they'll want to trap you, swallow you, incapacitate you in some way because they're afraid of you. And they'll want to do the same to me."

"Can't Hades just explain to them…"

"There's no time. You need to leave the Underworld and fly to Selene. Tell her I sent you. Ask her to hide you."

"You want me to fly?"

Hecate grabbed Ellie by the wrist and pulled her across the room, where she opened a wooden door. "This is the back way out of the palace. Turn right and follow the River of Fire. It will lead you to the gate."

"What about Fluffy?" Ellie asked.

"Who?"

"The big dog with the three heads."

"Cerberus. Just fly past him as fast as you can," Hecate said. "He's more concerned with those coming in than those going out, so you should be fine if you're fast about it."

Ellie did not feel reassured.

"Try to be as inconspicuous as possible," Hecate added. "Zeus's spies are everywhere. Now hurry! As fast as you can!"

Hecate shoved Ellie through the door and into the winding, cavernous tunnel.

When she spotted the river of fire, Ellie began to run, but her feet moved so much faster than she was used to, and she tripped and fell on her face.

Surprisingly enough, it hadn't hurt much. And, although there was blood on her hand when she wiped her chin, the next time she wiped it, the cut had healed.

Hearing voices somewhere off in the distance, Ellie took off running again, this time doing a better job of it. On the other side of the river of fire, she heard screaming. When she glanced in that direction, she thought she saw a woman with snake-like hair and bloody eyes sitting on top of another person. *That must be hell,* Ellie thought as she kept running.

She knew she was going the right way when she passed the stone building where Hecate had parked the chariot, and beyond that was the river the old man on the raft had come in on. The gate should be just beyond it, but to cross the river, she would need to swim or fly.

In the next instant, the old man on the raft came into view. Even though he was still several yards away, she could see him clearly, as if looking through binoculars. He was squinting at her suspiciously.

"Who are you?" he called out to her.

Ellie jumped into the air and flailed her arms and legs and was shocked when she didn't fall. She flew clumsily over the old man and his raft directly toward the tall iron gate. She could see the three-headed creature standing menacingly on the other side. Picking up speed, she nearly hit the top of the gate, spinning wildly in the wrong direction before managing to correct herself, all the while hollering out, "Whoa!"

Be inconspicuous, Ellie, she reminded herself.

The three-headed dog heard her cries and growled ferociously as she flew toward him. Once she was overhead, all three jaws snapped at her, nearly catching one of her feet.

She'd barely slipped past the three-headed dog when she noticed the narrow crevice ahead. *How had two horses and a chariot fit through?* she wondered.

Anxious about wasting too much time, Ellie steeled herself and went for it. With surprising dexterity and reflexes, Ellie maneuvered though the narrow crevice and out into the dark night in a matter of seconds. Now all she needed was to find Selene.

Without hesitating, Ellie soared up toward the clouds, searching for the bright silver chariot that regular people thought was a solid orb called the moon. Before she breached the clouds, however, she was surprised by the descent of a golden chariot. It was headed right for her. How could the other gods have discovered her so quickly?

As she was about to turn away, she caught a glimpse of the passengers. She didn't recognize the female driver, but behind her were three gods she knew. Her heart rejoiced at the sight of them.

"Phobos! Deimos!" she hollered. "Cupid! It's me! Ellie!"

Phobos sat in the middle. He and Deimos both had the sexy, rugged look of men who haven't shaved for a few days. Although their blue eyes were bright, there was something different about the twins. They appeared haggard and worn out, like they'd come down with the flu. Even Cupid looked ill.

"I'm so happy to see you," she said as the chariot neared and slowed to a halt. Then, when she saw their grim and cold expressions, her stomach dropped, and her throat was suddenly tight. "Oh, my gods, are you okay? Has something happened?"

"Get in," the driver said, motioning to the seat beside her.

Ellie climbed beside the driver and said, "I'm Ellie. It's nice to meet you."

The goddess ignored her.

Ellie turned to face the others. "Where are we going?"

"Who did this to you?" Cupid asked.

Ellie was afraid she'd get Hecate into trouble if she told them.

"Pretty cool, huh?" Ellie said with a smile. "We can talk about it later. What's going on? Has something happened? You look upset."

"I'll tell you what's happened," Phobos snarled. "Because of you, our powers have been stripped."

Ellie's mouth fell open. "What? How?"

"It's a long story," Cupid said. "Suffice it to say that we're being punished with six months of manual labor on a ranch in Texas."

"Because of me?" Ellie asked. "I'm so sorry." She wondered if she could do anything to make it up to them. "Maybe I can go with you and help."

"Please don't," Deimos said with a sigh. "You've already done enough."

"Why are you mad at *me*?" Ellie asked. "I didn't *try* to get you in trouble. It's not *my* fault the gods wanted to kill me. And I never asked you to protect me."

It suddenly dawned on Ellie what had happened. She turned to Cupid. "You shot them with arrows of hate."

"Ding, ding, ding, ding, ding!" Phobos said sarcastically. "Winner!"

"And the arrows worked," Deimos said. "So, there's no reason for you to come around us anymore."

"Cupid, how could you?" Ellie asked as tears pricked her eyes. "Is there any way to change them back?"

"I could shoot them with arrows of love again, but I'm without my powers," he said. "Besides, I'd never bond you to them both, and I'd never do it without their consent."

"He's never getting my consent," Phobos said.

"Nor mine," Deimos added.

Ellie couldn't believe that all the weeks they'd shared together meant nothing to them now. "I became immortal for *you*. I did this, so I could be with *you*—one of you, at least—forever."

"And now we can all live an eternity in misery," Deimos said harshly.

"I won't—I can't—give up on you," Ellie said. "I'll find a way to remind you how you once felt about me."

"You said it yourself," Phobos said. "We never *really* loved you. It was the arrow. What makes you think we'd love you without it?"

He had a point. Even though she was a goddess now and perfect in almost every way, there was no guarantee that either twin would develop feelings for her without Cupid's arrow. And, although it occurred to her that there might be a way to pull out the arrows of hate, Ellie knew she could never be truly happy with them if they couldn't fall in love with her on their own, without Cupid's help.

"What have I done?" she murmured as tears slipped down her cheeks.

"I'm truly sorry," Cupid said. "I never meant for any of this to happen."

"I know," she said through her tears. "You were only trying to help me. I know that, and I don't blame you. This is my fault. I was stupid for believing in an impossible dream." She wouldn't claim a purpose. She'd hide out with Selene for three months and then return to her mortal life. There was no point in living forever without Phobos and Deimos. Eternity would be so very lonely without them. "I'm gonna go now."

"No, you aren't," the goddess beside her said as she shoved an arrow through Ellie and pinned her to the chariot.

Before Ellie could pull the arrow out and make her escape, the goddess wound a massive chain around Ellie's wrists and ankles, moving nearly at the speed of light.

"You're coming with me," the goddess said.

"What are you doing, Artemis?" Cupid asked from the backseat.

"We're going back to Mount Olympus."

CHAPTER TWENTY-THREE

The Reckoning

Cupid couldn't feel guiltier for what he'd done to Ellie and his brothers, and the fact that Ellie didn't blame him for any of it made him feel worse. As Artemis steered the chariot toward Mount Olympus, Cupid felt uneasy about what the future held for Ellie. In his current state, there was nothing he could do. He'd never felt so helpless.

"Artemis," he said as they neared the gates. "She's committed no crime. Let her go."

"If her fate weren't bound to mine, I would," Artemis said. "Self-preservation is my priority. It should be yours as well."

"If it had been," Phobos said beside him, "we wouldn't be in this mess."

Artemis called out to the four seasons to open the gates and let them in. The clouds lifted, the gates parted, and the chariot entered. Artemis stopped the horses in the middle of the courtyard, grabbed her prisoner by the chains, and said, "Everyone out and follow me."

Stripped of their powers, Cupid and his brothers had no choice but to obey.

As they ascended the rainbow steps toward the great hall, Ellie craned her neck to look at Cupid and ask, "What's going to happen to me?"

"I don't know," he said.

He knew it wouldn't be good. Perhaps the Olympians would throw her into the Titan Pit to spend eternity with the rest of their enemies.

When they reached the great hall, most of the gods were still there. Hermes was gone—probably looking for Hecate—and Demeter and Persephone had likely retired to their rooms. Aphrodite sat weeping on her throne surrounded by her Graces, who consoled her as best they could. Ares stood beside Zeus and Hera in conversation. Athena was talking with Hephaestus. Apollo and Poseidon seemed to be arguing.

As Cupid, Artemis, and her other prisoners crossed the threshold into the great hall, all eyes turned on them.

Zeus stood up, eyebrows disappearing beneath his curly brown hair. "What's this?"

The hall became filled with gasps as one god after another realized that Ellie had been made a god.

"Who did this to you?" Poseidon demanded.

The lord of the Underworld appeared in the center of the room with his helm in his hand. "I did."

Sounds of surprise filled the room. Demeter and Persephone entered from their chambers, curious to learn what had happened.

"Hello, darling," Hades said to his wife.

"Hades? What have you done?" Persephone asked.

"I've saved Mount Olympus. You can thank me later."

"You better have a logical explanation for this, Hades," Zeus said.

"I have a logical explanation for everything I do," Hades said.

"You've got our attention," Poseidon said. "Start explaining."

"I know what you all think of me," Hades said. "You think I'm a liar, the kind of god who would hurt his own family if it suited his needs."

"What has that got to do with anything?" Zeus asked.

"Everything," Hades said. "Because I believe you and the other Olympians have projected your guilt onto me, unfairly. And if there's anything I can't stand, it's injustice."

"What are you blabbering on about?" Poseidon asked. "I don't understand a word you've said."

"The reckoning," Hades said.

Cupid glanced at his mother, who still had tears in her eyes. A glance at his father showed a different expression: anger.

"What about it?" Zeus asked.

"Ellie Beaufort was sent to us as a test," Hades said. "And you would have failed if it hadn't been for me."

"How did you come to know this?" Apollo asked.

"I don't *know* it," Hades said. "Only the Fates can know for certain what the future holds. But it's a damn good guess. Think about it. What is a reckoning? It's a time to evaluate, a time to appraise, a time to judge. Who knows more about Judgment Day than I?"

Poseidon scoffed. "Can you please stop talking in riddles and get to the point?"

"The Fates hold us accountable," Hades said. "Just as I do the mortals who come to my realm. I believe the Fates sent Apollo that vision to see what we would do with the mortal girl. Would we protect her, since we created her, even at our own peril; or, would we try to save our own hides and destroy her?"

Athena stepped forward. "It is for the mortals that we must preserve Mount Olympus. Without us, they couldn't survive."

"See, that's not true, Athena." Hades wagged a finger at her. "You're lying to yourself. The mortals need deities, sure, but those deities don't need to be us. If Mount Olympus fell, the Titans would rise. There would always be another pantheon to take the place of ours."

"You think the Titans would preserve the human race?" Hera smirked.

"They could do no worse than gods who continuously put their self-preservation first," Hades argued.

Cupid glanced at Artemis, whose face had turned the color of rubies. She refused to meet his gaze.

Zeus's face was just as red when he struck the air with a fist and shouted, "How dare you insult this entire court? Instead of working behind our backs, you should have consulted with us."

"You made up your mind the moment you heard the prophecy what your solution would be," Hades accused. "There was nothing anyone could have said to change your mind, especially me."

"We'll never know, will we?" Poseidon said.

"I'll tell you another thing we won't know," Zeus began. "We won't know if immortalizing Ellie was the very thing that would bring us crashing down. Hades guessed that saving her life was the answer. But what if her apotheosis is the threat?"

"I won't declare my purpose," Ellie murmured.

All eyes turned to Artemis's prisoner.

"I don't want to remain immortal." Ellie glanced at Phobos and Deimos, who stood on one side of her. "There's no longer a reason to."

Cupid was surprised to see a hint of sympathy cross the faces of some of the gods. They were moved to pity.

Ellie said, "If you want to kill me in three months, when I go back to being mortal, be my guest."

Hades shook his head. "Preemptive murder when we don't have all the facts is never a good idea. I'm telling you as someone who deals in justice every single day: we must take the high moral ground if we're to survive the reckoning."

Apollo stood up. "Hades is right when he says that we don't have all the facts. I suggest we postpone making a decision about the future of Ellie Beaufort until we know more."

"Who knows how long that could take?" Hephaestus complained.

"And what do we do with Ellie in the meantime?" Athena asked.

"I have an idea." Hera stood beside Zeus. "I can think of no better punishment for Cupid and his brothers in their blatant disrespect for this court than to strip the new goddess of her temporary powers and send her to the same Texas ranch to work alongside the very gods who despise her."

Hades crossed his arms and pulled at his beard. "That seems hardly fair to Ellie, whose done nothing disrespectful to this court other than to exist."

"There may be a lesson in this for Hades, too," Poseidon said. "I like the idea."

Hera smiled.

Zeus put an arm around his wife's waist. "All those in favor of stripping Ellie Beaufort of her powers and condemning her for six months, or until she reverts to her mortal form, on the same Texas ranch as the others, say aye."

The hall echoed with the word of consent.

"All those opposed?" Zeus asked.

Hades cried, "Nay," but his vote alone wasn't enough to affect the verdict.

Ellie was cold and miserable in the front of the chariot with Artemis as they flew from one side of the world to the other—from darkness in the east to high noon in the west, where Helios's cup sailed directly overhead. Knowing that Phobos and Deimos hated her made Ellie feel even more miserable and alone.

But it didn't prevent Ellie from glancing back at them one too many times. She tried to be inconspicuous by pretending she was watching a bird or studying something in the landscape below them. Deimos ignored her altogether. Phobos glared at her every single time.

Even without their powers, without their godly radiance, they were beautiful to her. And knowing what she knew didn't change the fact that she was still in love with them. She couldn't fault them for how they felt about her. How could she? They had been pawns in this game of the gods just as much as she had.

As miserable and cold as Ellie was feeling, she also felt a new sense of hope. When she'd first heard Hera's idea of sending Ellie to work with Phobos and Deimos, she'd nearly jumped for joy and had to bite her tongue to prevent herself from begging the other gods to agree. And when the gods *had* agreed to send her, Ellie had to bite her tongue even harder to prevent herself from smiling.

The truth was that it had been the idea of living without them that had led her to the brink of giving up. Now, whether they liked it or not, Phobos and Deimos were stuck with her for at least three months, and possibly longer, if she changed her mind and decided to declare a purpose. She would use that time wisely. She would not waste a single moment. Ellie would do everything in her power to make those boys fall in love with her again.

Artemis pulled up along a dirt road off the main highway and brought the chariot to a halt.

"We'll walk from here," Artemis said. "Follow me."

The goddess had taken but a few steps when she stopped, turned around, and made the chariot invisible to mortal eyes—and to gods whose powers had been stripped. Then she gave each of the boys a once over and snapped her finger. Their trousers became blue jeans, their shoes became cowboy boots, and their button-down Oxford shirts became plaid.

Ellie's eyes felt like they could pop from their sockets. She hadn't thought it possible for Phobos and Deimos to look any hotter.

"That's better," Artemis said. "Now you'll fit in."

"What about me?" Ellie, who was still wearing the lavender blouse, jeans, and flat-heeled boots from Hecate, asked.

"You look fine," she said.

"Can't I at least have a pair of cowboy boots?" Ellie asked.

Artemis rolled her eyes but acquiesced.

Ellie liked the way they looked on her. She gave the twins a flirty glance, but they ignored her.

They continued down the dirt road. It wound uphill and across a pond to a farmhouse on a hill.

The house looked old with rotten siding, one broken window, and two missing shutters. There was a front porch, but it was filled with junk—an old mattress, a broken baby stroller, an empty ice chest, an old refrigerator, and a few cardboard boxes filled with more junk.

Artemis stepped up to the front door and knocked.

An old man opened the door. "Hola, Artemis. Cómo está?

"You two know each other?" Ellie blurted out.

"Why yes," the old man said. "Artemis has been hunting on my land for…I don't know how many years."

"A very long time," Artemis said with a friendly smile.

"If it weren't for her business," the man continued, "I would've gone broke a long time ago."

"I brought you some desperados," Artemis said. "These parolees need to do community service for six months. I used my connections to get them sent here, to work for you, in exchange for room and board and no wages. I remembered you had that old shack out back. They can stay there."

"I don't know about that shack, mija," the old man said. "It's falling apart."

"That can be their first job," Artemis said. "They can repair it."

"They're handy?" the man asked.

"Very," Artemis said. "And Cupid here—that's his nickname—he's an expert horse handler."

The man's face brightened. "Wonderful! Oh, that's exactly what we need around here."

"Does that mean you'll take them?" Artemis asked.

"Of course, mija. Of course. Muchas gracias. My wife will be so pleased. It's hard for her with the grandchildren, since their mother passed away, you know."

"I know, Mr. Garcia. I know," Artemis said with a sympathetic smile. "Let me introduce you."

After introductions had been made, Artemis led Ellie and the boys to the shack.

Ellie was glad that the Garcias had remained at the farmhouse, because it gave her the freedom to say, "Are you serious? You expect us to *live* here?"

"Other people have," Artemis said. "You can, too."

"Come on," Phobos argued. "This place is a dump."

"What if it rains?" Cupid wondered.

"I have a feeling you'll survive," Artemis said as she opened the rickety front door. "Come on inside. There are two bedrooms with two bunks each. Cupid and Ellie will sleep there, and Phobos and Deimos over there. There's an outhouse out back, and you saw the well. We passed it on the way over here from the house."

Deimos shook his head "No indoor plumbing. Just great."

"You'll eat your meals in the farmhouse," Artemis said. "Breakfast at six, lunch at noon, and supper at eight."

"This bedding is filthy," Ellie said of the sheets and blankets on the bunks.

"You know where the well is," Artemis said. "Ask for some soap and launder them."

As flabbergasted as Ellie was by the state of their living quarters, even the lack of indoor plumbing couldn't extinguish her feelings of excitement and hope.

"Now here's a bag for each of you," Artemis said. "You have a change of clothes and toiletries."

"One change of clothes?" Phobos asked. "You expect us to wash our clothes each day?"

"You'll manage," Artemis said. "But pray to me if there's something you can't fix on your own. I may or may not respond."

"Great," Cupid said.

Just then, Mr. Garcia entered. "I'm sorry it's not much."

"It'll be just fine," Artemis said.

"We'll make the best of it," Ellie said with a light heart. "Won't we, guys?"

Phobos and Deimos glared at her, but Ellie didn't let that get her down.

THE END

Thank you for reading my story. If you enjoyed it, please consider leaving a review. Reviews help other readers to find my books, which helps me.

Please enjoy the first chapter of the next book in the series, *Phobos*.

The Shack

I don't know what Artemis was thinking, sending us here with flannel shirts," Deimos complained inside the dilapidated shack they would call home for the next six months. "It's too damn hot."

Phobos had already stripped his off, preferring to go without a shirt altogether than to spend one more miserable second wearing what felt like a wet blanket. "Preach, brother."

Cupid dug through the bag Artemis had given each of them. "Thank the gods, there's a clean t-shirt in here." He whipped off the flannel and pulled on the white t-shirt, grinning with relief.

Deimos followed suit. "Amen, brother. This is much better."

Cupid's brows flew up. "So, you *have* forgiven me?"

"We're going to be trapped here together for six months," Deimos said. "I'd rather not make it worse."

"What about you, Phobos?" Cupid asked as he folded the flannel shirt and returned it to the bag.

"Give me time."

Cupid frowned and nodded. "Of course."

Phobos noticed Ellie standing in the corner, enjoying the show.

He crossed the room and glared down at her. "What are you looking at?"

Her eyes roamed across his bare chest before she met his gaze. "I'm going to the well to wash my bedding. Would you like me to wash yours, too?"

"I don't want you anywhere near my bedding," Phobos said.

He could tell by her expression that his words had stung. Good.

She stepped back and turned to his brothers. "Deimos? Cupid? Can I wash your bedding?"

"Thanks, Ellie," Cupid said. "That's very kind of you."

"I'm good," Deimos said without looking at her.

Phobos groaned when Cupid followed Ellie to their room, offering to help her. He wondered who would take the top bunk and who the bottom. Phobos had already called dibs on the bottom bunk in the five-by-seven-foot "bedroom" he shared with Deimos. To Phobos, "closet" seemed like a better word. Even the closet in his London flat was bigger.

The entire shack was no more than twelve feet by twelve feet.

He supposed being stuck with Ellie and his brothers in the Texas heat in a falling-down shack without indoor plumbing or electricity was better than being condemned to the Titan Pit.

But not by much.

Because he was accustomed to sensing people—both gods and mortals—before they announced themselves, he was startled by a knock at the door. His lack of powers was unnerving. This was going to be an agonizingly long six months.

They'd left the door ajar, because of the heat, and the person knocking there was fully visible. It was a young woman carrying a deep plastic tub, a broom, and a lantern. She had long brown hair pulled back from her face with a clip. Her brown eyes were round and lined with dark, thick lashes. Her brows were thick, too, which Phobos found sexy. She was smiling up at him. Maybe things weren't going to be so bad here, after all.

"Hi," she said. "I'm Jaquelyn. My parents told me to bring you these."

"Come in," Phobos said.

She was wearing denim cut-offs and a t-shirt with the letters YOLO printed on it. By his estimation, she looked to be about seventeen.

Jaquelyn set the tub down on the rickety old table on one side of the room. "I have some canteens for each of you. It's important to stay hydrated."

"It's ridiculously hot here," Deimos said. "I'm sure those will come in handy."

"Yeah, August is the worst," Jaquelyn said. "Plan to swim every day to keep from dying of heatstroke."

Phobos lifted his brows. "That sounds nice. I saw a big pond on the way in."

"My parents would rather you not swim there," Jaquelyn said as her cheeks turned pink.

"Then where?" Phobos asked, already missing his spa on Mount Olympus.

"In the streams. Just watch out for Rusty, our bull, if you swim in the northeast pasture. He shouldn't bother you but be aware that he's there."

"Got it," Deimos said. "And where is the northeast pasture from here?"

"My dad's coming by in about an hour to give you a tour. He wanted me to bring this stuff down, so you could get settled first."

Deimos offered Jaquelyn his hand. "I'm Deimos. It's nice to meet you, Jaquelyn."

She shook it. "Likewise."

Phobos offered his. "Phobos."

Cupid entered with a bundle of bedding in his arms, followed by Ellie.

"Hi," Cupid said. "I'm Cupid, and this is Ellie."

"Hello," Ellie said.

"Hi." Jaquelyn gave her a smile. "I've seen you before, on television. Aren't you a pitcher for the Seminoles?"

Ellie blushed. "I was. A lot has happened since then."

"But it's only been two months since you won the world series," Jaquelyn pointed out.

"Do you play?" Ellie asked.

"I wish. I used to, but not anymore."

"That's too bad," Ellie said.

Jaquelyn averted her eyes. "I was just telling Phobos and Deimos that my dad will be down to give you a tour of the ranch in about an hour. My parents sent this tub of things to help you get settled. There's a toolbox in here from my dad. And my mom sent some cleaning supplies and rags, if you want to wipe this place down."

"Oh, good," Ellie said. "And you brought a broom. The floors could use a good sweeping."

"Yeah," Jaquelyn said. "No one's used this place in a few years."

Phobos fought the urge to say it looked like it hadn't been used in a few *decades*.

"I've also brought a box of laundry detergent, bars of soap, two bottles of shampoo, and four clean towels," Jaquelyn added. "And I guess you saw the well on your way over. You can use it for drinking and for clean water to wash yourselves and your clothes and bedding. That's what this big tub is for—for washing and rinsing. Just be sure to dump the soapy water away from the animals."

"Thank you," Phobos said. He'd never had to launder a thing in his life, but he reminded himself that there were worse fates.

"You're welcome to use the clothesline across from the well to dry your things. We have a washer and dryer and rarely use the clothesline anymore."

"Thanks," Cupid said.

"So, you want us to bathe at the well?" Ellie asked.

Jaquelyn's cheeks turned pink again. "Only when you want to use soap and shampoo. We'd rather you not use chemicals in the streams, since the animals drink from them."

Phobos could tell that Ellie wasn't happy about that.

"Oh, and there's an outhouse under the tree over there—I'm not sure if you saw it. It's for when you need to go at night. I brought you a flashlight, so you can find your way in the dark. You're welcome to use the restroom in the main house during the day."

"That's great news," Ellie said. "What a relief!"

Jaqueline laughed. "Hopefully, you won't have to use the outhouse at all."

"Especially if you avoid drinking at night," Cupid said.

"Which shouldn't be hard," Jaquelyn added with a laugh. "You'll be ready to crash after supper. Trust me."

Phobos had normally gone at least three days without sleep, but he'd also never had his powers stripped from him. Now that he thought about it, he could use a nap.

"Just in case you want to read or hang out before bed, here's a lantern," Jaqueline said.

"Awesome. Thanks," Cupid said.

"We have breakfast at six, lunch at noon, and supper at eight. Mom told me to tell you she's planning on feeding you this evening."

"We look forward to it," Deimos said.

"Well, it was nice meeting you all." Jaquelyn turned to the door. "I'm sorry we don't have a nicer place for you to stay in."

Phobos noticed her glance at his bare chest. He'd been hoping she would. He'd begun to believe she was more interested in Ellie than in him or his brothers, but that glance, and her awkward smile when she knew she was caught, had told him otherwise.

"Thank you," Phobos said. "I suppose we'll be seeing a lot of each other."

"Yep. See you."

Phobos watched her walk away, past the well, and back to the main house. Cupid followed with his bundle of bedding. Ellie emptied the tub of everything but the laundry detergent and used it to carry her bedding as she followed Cupid to the well. Phobos was surprised when Ellie didn't look back at him. As much as he despised her, he'd taken a sick kind of pleasure in watching her long for him. His heart could feel both arrows compelling him to hate and to love, but the hate won out. Had Ellie given up already?

"I saw the way you were looking at Jaquelyn," Deimos said, bringing Phobos from his thoughts.

"So?"

"Try not to make things worse."

"Worse?" Phobos scoffed. "How could they possibly get worse? I'd say a pretty girl makes things better."

"Like it did with Ellie?" Deimos snapped.

"That was different."

"You could still break her heart."

"Ellie's? Why should I care? Do you?"

"Jaquelyn's."

Phobos dug through the bag from Artemis and found a white t-shirt. He didn't want to hurt the mortal, but he needed something to lift him from this misery. The hate he felt for Ellie was overwhelming. Every time he looked at her, he wanted to slap her, crush her, hurt her. He knew it was the arrow of hate that was driving his hatred, but it was powerful and all-consuming, no matter how much he tried to reason with himself.

Even when he focused on the memories that he'd made with her—of kissing her mouth and throat in Selene's cave, of touching her breasts in Cupid's swimming pool, of kneading her between the legs on Circe's island—they only further fueled his hatred. The only thing that made him feel better was knowing that she ached for him and couldn't have him.

Cupid pumped water into the plastic tub while Ellie added some detergent. Then they sat on the stone ledge around the pump with the tub between them and scrubbed the bedding.

Ellie looked around, finding the place wasn't as bad as she had originally thought. The farmhouse was prettier from the back. If the Garcia family were to clean off their front porch, it would make a huge difference, in her opinion. Replacing the rotten siding, missing shutters, and broken window in the front would do wonders as well.

The family kept everything tidy in the back. The dirt driveway that ran in a straight line from the side of the house to the barn divided the area into two sides. The farmhouse, well, clothesline, shack and outhouse were on the west side of it, while the garage, chicken coop, pens, and stables were on the east. Pea gravel covered the ground and most of the driveway.

Everything in the back was utilitarian—nothing fancy. But the front had been beautiful until you reached the front porch and saw the junk in front of the worn-down farmhouse. The dirt road had curved from the main road around a stack of boulders on the left, over a large pond, and past a garden on the right. The road had curved again in front of the house, in a semicircle, before splitting two ways: if you went straight, you would go into the garage. If you turned left, you would drive past the house, the well, and the shack and into the barn.

Ellie imagined what the farmhouse would look like with repairs and fresh paint.

"A penny for your thoughts," Cupid said.

"I was just thinking how pretty this place is, now that the shock of coming here has worn off."

"It's hard to see the beauty when it's so damn hot." Cupid washed his face with some of the water and allowed it to drip down his neck.

"It's the hottest time of the day. Hopefully it'll cool down this evening."

"The shack isn't much, is it," Cupid said without inflection. "Three plain rooms."

"It's certainly not your castle." Ellie laughed.

Cupid laughed, too. "Yeah. It's a little different."

"I doubt we'll be spending much time in it."

"At least it has a lot of windows. I opened them up first thing, to get the air circulating."

"But no screens. I hope we won't get eaten alive by mosquitoes."

"I hadn't thought of that."

"Check out that chicken coop. I wonder if we'll wake up to roosters singing cock-a-doodle-do in the morning."

"Gods, I hope not." Cupid wrung out the excess water from the bedding. "If you'll hold the sheets and blankets, I'll pour out this soapy water and pump in some clean water for rinsing."

Ellie bundled the bedding in her arms while Cupid walked across the gravel and dumped the water near the fence behind the outhouse.

After they'd rinsed the soap out of the bedding, they worked together to hang the sheets, blankets, and pillowcases on the line. They were finishing up when Phobos and Deimos joined them with their bedding rolled up in their arms.

Ellie smiled at them, but Deimos avoided her eyes, and Phobos glared at her.

Without saying a word, she followed Cupid to the shack, where she got to work dusting, wiping up cobwebs, and sweeping all the floors, while Cupid took out each of the mattresses and pillows and beat them against a tree. It hadn't taken long to tidy up the place, because it was so small. Ellie was organizing their supplies in a set of cabinets opposite the table and chairs when the twins returned with Cupid, the plastic tub, and the last of the mattresses.

She'd been hoping they'd remark on the shack's transformation in the short time they'd been out, but after they helped Cupid return the mattress to its bunk, they each sat on one of the four wooden chairs around the table and said nothing. So, after organizing the supplies and putting away the wash bin, Ellie retreated to her and Cupid's room to put the few clothes, toothbrush, and hairbrush Artemis had given her on the shelves in the tiny closet. Then she sat on the bottom bunk, put her hands in her face, and cried.

Phobos stood in the doorway of her room. "What are you blubbering about?"

"What do you think?"

"*You* grew up living in poverty. Think how hard this is for the *rest* of us."

She furrowed her brows. "You really think *that's* why I'm crying?"

Phobos frowned.

"Just go away and leave me alone," she said.

"I came to tell you that the rancher is here and wants to give us the tour."

Ellie wiped her eyes and sniffed as she stood from the lower bunkbed. She didn't like the way Phobos was watching her, as if he took pleasure in her pain. She missed the man who would do anything to make her feel safe and loved, who'd tell the corniest jokes to offset the impact he had on her as the god of fear.

She recalled the first time she'd met Deacon, the satyr, and how she had grabbed Phobos's arm in fear. Phobos had made her laugh by saying that for once he wasn't the scariest thing in the room. When Deacon had sarcastically said, "You're hilarious," Phobos had turned to her and had said, "I told you."

Thinking about that moment now made her giggle as she followed Phobos from the room.

He glanced back at her. "What's so funny?"

"Something you said a couple of months ago. I miss the days when you used to make me laugh."

Phobos said nothing in reply as he joined his brothers at the door, where Mr. Garcia was waiting.

228

Eva Pohler is a *USA Today* bestselling author of over thirty novels in multiple genres, including mysteries, thrillers, and young adult paranormal romance based on Greek mythology. Her books have been described as "addictive" and "sure to thrill"—*Kirkus Reviews*.

To learn more about Eva and her books, and to sign up to hear about new releases, and sales, please visit her website at www.evapohler.com.